A PAGE TURNER BOOKSHOP

The Willowbrook Series
Book 2

By Laura Landon

ARE YOU SIGNED UP FOR DRAGONBLADE'S BLOG?

You'll get the latest news and information on exclusive giveaways, exclusive excerpts, coming releases, sales, free books, cover reveals and more.

Check out our complete list of authors, too!

No spam, no junk. That's a promise!

Sign Up Here

www.dragonbladepublishing.com

Dearest Reader;

Thank you for your support of a small press. At Dragonblade Publishing, we strive to bring you the highest quality Historical Romance from some of the best authors in the business. Without your support, there is no 'us', so we sincerely hope you adore these stories and find some new favorite authors along the way.

Happy Reading!

CEO, Dragonblade Publishing

**Additional Dragonblade books by
Author Laura Landon**

The Willowbrook Series
A Willowbrook Miracle (Book 1)
A Page Turner Bookshop (Book 2)

Men of Valor Series
A Love For All Time (Book 1)
A Love That Knows No Bounds (Book 2)
A Love That's Worth The Risk (Book 3)
A Love That Heals the Heart (Book 4)

CHAPTER ONE

ETHAN ESSEX TOOK the back stairs to the queen's private receiving room and entered her antechamber. The hall was cloaked in semidarkness to conceal late-night visitors from being observed.

"Are you here to see Her Majesty on royal business?" Rupert Blackheart asked, stepping out of the shadows. Ethan had reached the end of the shadowy hall, and only then did Blackheart make himself known.

Ethan wasn't sure what title to assign to Rupert Blackheart. He might be called an advisor to the queen, but Ethan wouldn't go so far as to call him a "trusted" advisor. He was simply someone who always followed Her Majesty around like a shadow. He followed her wherever she went. He'd even heard Her Majesty ask Blackheart's opinion on an occasional matter. But he'd never heard Her Majesty follow his advice. If anything, she chose to do the opposite of whatever Blackheart advised.

"Yes," Ethan answered.

"Was your mission completed successfully?"

"Yes."

Blackheart walked to the door to the anteroom. "I'll see if Her Majesty will see you," he said, then stepped inside the room.

Ethan propped his back against the wall, then bent at the waist and anchored his hands on his thighs. He didn't remember being so tired since after a battle during the war. He straightened and raked his fingers through his hair. He was so tired he could barely keep his eyes open, and his temper was frayed to a thin thread. He just wanted to go to bed and sleep for a week.

He thought back to what Blackheart had said. Of course Her Majesty would see him. Who did this conceited popinjay think he was? The queen was the one who'd sent him on this assignment, issuing the command that he return with news of the result the second the assignment was completed. It was her edict that had forced him to ride day and night for the last two days to reach London when he hadn't managed to get an hour of sleep in the last three days.

The door opened, and Blackheart held it. Instead of motioning for Ethan to enter the room that Her Majesty would meet him in, he stepped back. Her Majesty walked through the open doorway and came toward him.

He bowed, then kissed the queen's hand when she extended it.

"Mr. Essex."

"Your Majesty."

"I take it your assignment went well?"

"Yes, Your Majesty."

"Good."

The queen walked regally across the room and stopped before the door that led to a darkened hallway. Blackheart raced across the room and opened the door for her.

"Would you mind walking with me, Essex?"

"Of course, Your Majesty."

Ethan followed her out of the room, then stopped when she did. She turned to face Blackheart. "You stay here, Blackheart. I won't be long."

Ethan almost laughed at the shock and disappointment on Blackheart's face. This was probably the only time Her Majesty had ever gone anywhere without her shadow.

Ethan extended his arm, and Her Majesty placed her hand upon his sleeve.

"We will go in the room at the end of the hall on your left."

"Yes, Your Majesty."

When they reached the end room, Ethan opened the door and escorted her into the room. Three lanterns were lit—two on the mantel above a flickering fireplace, and one in the center of a table with two chairs positioned on each side. Ethan assisted Her Majesty into one of the chairs, then went to stand by the opposite chair.

"Please, check the doors and make sure we cannot be overheard, Essex."

"Yes, Your Majesty," Ethan answered, then went to each of the three doors to the room and checked to be certain no one was there.

"We are safe, Your Majesty," he said when he was done.

"Very good. Now would you pour me a whisky and claret, and help yourself to whatever you prefer."

Ethan went to the table that held several crystal decanters and poured Her Majesty a small glass of rich, red claret, to which he added a splash of whisky, and poured one for himself. He carried the glasses back to the table, then watched for Her Majesty's regal nod that would indicate he was to sit.

When it came, Ethan sat, then waited until the queen took a sip of her whisky before sampling his own.

"I assume your task went without incident?" she inquired.

"Yes, Your Majesty. Would you like to hear the details?"

"No, Essex. There's no need. I have enough confidence in you to know that everything went perfectly."

Ethan lowered his gaze. He was a perfectionist. Therefore, there would not be any mistakes. His kills were always clean.

"There is something else I need to speak to you about."

Ethan took another swallow of the good Scotch whisky, then placed his glass on the table and leaned back in his chair to listen.

"I have discovered that there is a traitor on the Finance Committee."

"Do you know who it is?" Ethan asked.

"Yes. At least, I've had reports of who it is."

"But you are not sure?"

"I've been assured of his identity. I simply have a hard time believing this particular person would do something so treasonous."

"What exactly is happening?"

"Accounts are being created that call for amounts of money to be paid into them. Not large amounts, but amounts that would hardly be noticed."

"How were these amounts discovered?"

"Quite by accident. The chief financial officer took on two young clerks to help him when there was a vacancy on the committee, and one of them discovered the errors."

"How long has this been going on?"

"Years," the queen answered.

Ethan's eyebrows rose. "The amount they have amassed must be astronomical."

"More than one hundred thousand pounds."

Ethan brought his glass to his mouth and took a swallow of his whisky. "Whoever managed to elude discovery for that long must be a mathematical genius."

"This is why I tend to question the validity of what the informant revealed, as well as the name of the person behind the theft. Although everything points to his guilt, I need to make sure of it. And I don't want his crime to become public knowledge."

"What orders are you giving, then, Your Majesty?"

"I don't want word of this to get out. To save his family's reputation, I don't want the public to discover what treasonous act he committed. I want his death to look like an accident, or a robbery gone wrong."

"Yes, Your Majesty," Ethan answered. "Drawing attention to the theft will cause insurmountable notoriety. It will stay in the papers for months."

"I agree with you, Essex," the queen responded. "And that is something I want to avoid if at all possible."

He thought back to the time in his family's history when his great-grandfather stole from the Crown in order to pay off his gambling debts. The Crown came down hard on his grandfather, as well as his family.

They lost the title that had been theirs for more than one hundred years. The land and the estate where they had lived was taken from them, and they were tossed out onto the street to make their way as best they could. Unable to bear the shame, Ethan's great-grandfather committed suicide and left his family to bear the brunt of the shame and embarrassment.

But rather than let the stigma of embarrassment define their future, Ethan's grandfather took his great love of books and used his passion as a way to support his mother and his young family. He opened a bookshop as a means to earn a living.

At first, very few customers stepped through the doors of the shop owned by a man whose father was a traitor to the Crown. But eventually, what Ethan's great-grandfather had done faded in people's memories, and by the time his father inherited the bookshop, very few people even remembered the black stain that marred his family name.

Ethan was glad this family would be spared the hardship and disgrace his family had endured. But it took until he was born for the black mark to fade.

"What are you thinking, Ethan?" Her Majesty asked.

He looked up into her face and saw clearly how anxious she was to avoid any hint of scandal. "So you doubt the guilt of the man accused of stealing from the Crown. Do you mind, then, if I verify his guilt before I act?"

"I would expect nothing less from someone with your standards."

"What is the name of the person who is being accused?"

"The Marquess of Springdale. He has a summer estate north of the village of Willowbrook. Perhaps you know of him?"

Ethan shook his head. "I'm afraid I do not. Although I haven't been in the area that long. I have, however, purchased a storefront there and have recently gone into business. I own my own bookshop—The Page Turner Bookshop."

The queen smiled. "You are to be commended, Essex. I would never have taken you as a lover of books."

"Anyone who knows me would never take me for an assassin."

"Even your family?" she asked.

"*Especially* my family. They could not even believe that I took a military commission in the middle of a war."

"There are many facets to you, aren't there, Ethan Essex?"

"I like to think so, Your Majesty."

Ethan started to rise, intending to escort her back to her suite, then stopped. "With your permission, Your Majesty, I would like to broach another subject."

"Yes?"

"With your permission, I would like to devote all my time and energy to making a success of my business. I have a replacement in mind to take over my duties to Your Majesty, but after this assignment, I beg you give me permission to leave your service."

"Are you sure you want to retire from government work?"

"Yes, Your Majesty. Quite sure. Killing isn't something I wish to continue doing."

The queen fingered her empty glass, then slid it away. "Are you sure there isn't anything I can say to change your mind, Essex?"

"No, Your Majesty. I wish to live the quiet life of a shop owner. That is what I want."

"Then I shall honor your wishes. You have served me and this country admirably for many years. I will give you over to your books." She rose a bit stiffly and waited for Ethan to offer his arm.

"Thank you, Your Majesty."

"You are welcome, Ethan Essex. You will inform me when your final assignment is finished."

"I will, Your Majesty."

The queen nodded, then stepped toward the door.

Ethan escorted her back to her room and left the palace. He only had this one assignment to carry out and he would be done killing.

CHAPTER TWO

ETHAN BROUGHT IN another box of books from the back room and opened it. Every time he got a new shipment of books, it was like opening presents on Christmas morning. This box contained an assortment of books by Jane Austen, Alexandre Dumas, Emily Bronte, and several other authors who wrote what most people referred to as *romance novels*.

Although they weren't favored by the male population, they were without doubt favorites of females. Especially books by Jane Austen and the Bronte sisters.

Ethan had begun putting the books on the shelf in an orderly fashion when the bell he'd installed above the door jingled. He looked toward the door, and his breath caught. One of the loveliest females he'd ever seen stood inside his shop.

She had hair the color of ripened wheat, and skin as clear and creamy as a porcelain doll. She wasn't overly tall—not enough that she towered over the shelves—just tall enough that she could peer above the books by standing on the tips of her toes.

She was dressed in a gown of a color Ethan would call mint green. She wore a matching bonnet that hid a great deal of her hair, but allowed several strands to escape and frame her heart-shaped face.

He wasn't sure what color her eyes were. He guessed blue, or green, but he'd have to see her up close to tell. And that was exactly what he intended to do.

"Hello, my lady," he called out from the back of the shop. He walked forward until he was closer to her.

Blue. Her eyes were blue. The clearest, most vibrant blue imaginable.

"May I help you find something?"

"Yes. I was looking for books by Jane Austen, or perhaps one of the Bronte sisters. Or perhaps a man called George Sand."

"If you will follow me," Ethan said, then led her to the back of his shop. He stopped when he reached the spot where the romance books were located. "I was just adding to my selection. Several new editions came in this morning, and I was trying to get them out."

"Oh, may I see them?" Her eyes shone with an excitement Ethan only saw in people who had a love for the written word.

"Here is my selection of Jane Austen novels. I keep multiple copies of these on hand, since Miss Austen is very popular. Here are the Bronte sisters' books. Any one of them is extremely popular. And here," he said, "is a book by George Sand. I only carry a limited supply of her books, since she is not as widely read."

"She? Don't you mean 'he'?"

"Actually no, my lady. George Sand is a pseudonym she uses to disguise the fact that she is a woman. I'm not exactly sure why," Ethan said.

"Oh," she exclaimed. "I didn't know that."

He smiled. "That's the purpose of using a pseudonym. So readers don't actually know who you are."

"Of course," she said, then laughed.

It was the loveliest sound Ethan had ever heard. Her laughter soared into his chest and wrapped around his heart like a soft, warm blanket. He was afraid she would choose one of the books he'd pointed out and leave, and he wasn't ready to be separated from her yet. He hadn't gazed into her midnight-blue eyes long enough, or memorized the lilt of her voice yet. He needed more time with her.

"Or, if you enjoy stories that have more adventure along with their romance, perhaps you would enjoy something by Alexandre Dumas. Have you read any of his works?" Ethan reached for a book that had just arrived.

"*The Count of Monte Cristo*," she said, cocking her head prettily to read the title. "Did you find it interesting?"

"I did. I thoroughly enjoyed it."

"Have you read all of the books in your shop?"

Ethan laughed. "Heavens no. I don't have the time or the patience to read everything I have in here. Although my father owns a bookshop in London, and I'd wager he's read nearly all the books in *his* shop. He asks me how I intend to recommend books to my customers if I haven't read them."

"I suppose he does have a point," she said. "But there are several books I simply don't have an interest in reading."

"I know. My answer to him was that I will wait until someone buys a book I prefer not to read, and the next time they come in I'll ask them what they thought of the book, and they can critique it so I don't have to read it."

"That's exactly what I would do," she said lightly.

Ethan watched her for a few more seconds, then the bell above the door rang and two more customers entered the shop. "If you will excuse me," he said. "I will let you look at some of the other books, and I'll wait on these ladies."

"Of course, Mr....?"

"Essex, my lady. Ethan Essex."

"Of course, Mr. Essex," she said as he turned to greet the two ladies who had entered the store.

He hadn't had an opportunity to make a proper introduction to the lady and ask for her name, but he would rectify that later. For there *would* be a later time. He was positive. He'd never met a woman who interested him as much as she did upon first meeting her.

Hopefully, there wouldn't be more customers in the shop

when she was ready to leave, and he could have an opportunity to ask her name. Until then, he'd simply think of her as...the beauty.

⟫⟫⟫⟫⟪⟪⟪⟪

UNFORTUNATELY, HIS BOOKSHOP was crowded all afternoon, and when the blue-eyed beauty brought her purchases—*The Count of Monte Cristo* and Charlotte Bronte's *Jane Eyre*—to the counter, there was a line of customers behind her. He didn't have an opportunity to ask her name, and she left before he could speak to her again. He admired her choices and made a mental note that she was not a light reader.

Ethan went back to the case of books he had yet to unpack and worked until he heard the bell above the door jingle again. He looked up, pleased to see his friend Hunter Malcome, Earl of Murdock, with his wife Victoria, Countess of Murdock.

"Welcome," Ethan called from the back of the store.

"What are you doing?" Hunt asked as he and Torie moved toward the stock room.

"I'm trying to get this case of books put on the shelves, but I've been so busy, I can't stay with it long enough to make any progress."

"That's a good problem to have, Ethan," Torie said, looking at the books he was unpacking.

"Yes, it is. But I think I'm going to have to hire someone to help me. Someone to stay behind the counter and wait on the customers so I can help the customers who need assistance and get some work done. All I get done is running back and forth."

"It's obvious you need someone to help you," Hunt said. "At least you'll have a chance to run to the sandwich shop and grab a bite for lunch."

"That reminds me—I haven't had time to eat yet today, and I'm famished."

"That's not good for you, Ethan," Torie said. "Hunt, why don't you run to the sandwich shop and bring back something for Ethan? And I wouldn't mind a little something, too."

"Are you still hungry?" Hunt said in a teasing tone. "I can't believe you can be hungry after the big lunch we had."

"Well, I am. Actually, I'm not. It's your son who is always hungry."

Hunt laughed, then leaned down and gave his wife a quick kiss. "Obviously our baby is a boy," he said as he left the bookshop.

"Of course he is. If I were having a girl, she wouldn't be nearly this hungry all the time. Now, go."

Ethan laughed as Hunt closed the door behind him. "So, how are you feeling, Torie?" he asked.

"I'm feeling fine, and even when I'm not, I can't let Hunt know I'm not, or he'd insist I go see Dr. Edwards every day."

"He's just concerned."

"I know," Torie said with a smile. "So, how is your business going, Ethan?"

"Remarkably well," he answered. "I had convinced myself that it would be slow at first, and it's anything but. There's hardly a time when I'm by myself."

"So, do you have any idea of someone to hire to help you?"

"No, I'm thinking about putting an ad in the paper and seeing who applies."

"Do you mind if I offer my suggestion?"

"Of course not, Torie. What do you think I should do?"

"What is your primary requirement for the person you're looking for?"

"Well, that he or she is well read and a lover of several different kinds of books," he replied.

"That would be my main requirement, too. And where are you going to find people who meet that requirement?"

"Right here," Ethan said. "Among the clientele that visit the bookshop. The clients who constantly come in my shop, sometimes simply to browse."

"Very wise. And may I also suggest the bookshops in London? Didn't you say that your father owned one?"

"Yes."

"Perhaps he would post an advertisement for you. You never know who might see your post and want to apply."

Ethan felt an enthusiasm he hadn't felt for a long time. "That's a wonderful idea, Torie. Those are the ideal places to post advertisements." He reached out, took Torie's hands, and brought them to his lips.

"What is this?" a voice said from the doorway. "I leave you alone with my wife for five minutes and I come back and find you kissing her."

Torie giggled. "Are you jealous, Hunt?"

"Well," Hunt said, bringing a small box of sandwiches, pastries, and drinks in and setting them on the counter, "I might be."

"You have nothing to be jealous about," she said. "I am as big as a barn, and no one would even look at me once, let alone twice."

"That's not true, is it, Ethan?"

"Definitely not, Hunt," Ethan replied. "Not only is your wife beautiful, but she's brilliant."

"What puzzle did she solve for you today, Ethan?"

"I told Torie that I need to look for someone to help me in the store. I'm finding I alone cannot handle the number of customers that come in demanding my attention, and she came up with the perfect solution."

"Of course. She would. She's good at that."

"Oh, Hunt," Torie said with a smile. "You are overflowing with compliments today."

"That's because you deserve them. You're an organizational mastermind."

Torie met Hunt's heart-stopping smile, and her cheeks darkened. She reached out and clasped her hand to his.

Hunt cleared his throat and turned to Ethan. "Come, let's sit down and eat the lunch I brought while there's a lull, and you can tell me what Torie came up with the perfect answer for."

"Gladly."

Their leisurely lunch in the supply room was the congenial sort of thing that was all too scarce in Ethan's life. He realized he'd been as hungry for companionship as he had been for the cold cuts Hunt had brought.

When they finished and Hunt and Torie left, Ethan sketched out the design for a poster advertising his need for an assistant. He put one of the advertisements in his bookshop, another in the small lending library that had just been started, and a third advertisement in the post and sent it to his father. Maybe, just maybe, someone would see his advertisement and apply for the position.

CHAPTER THREE

"WHERE ARE YOU going, Polly?" the Marquess of Springdale asked his daughter as she descended the stairs.

"I'm going to walk into Willowbrook, Papa. I want to look for a pink ribbon to match the new gown Madame Cartwright just made for me. Then I need to stop at the bookshop and buy another book."

"Have you read both of the books you came home with already? It hasn't been a week since you bought them."

"Do I need to watch how much I spend, Papa?"

Polly knew all she needed to do was question his ability to provide funds, and her father would rush to tell her that money wasn't a problem. That he had more than enough to pay for anything she might want or need.

"No, sweetheart. You can buy whatever you want. I just thought you might want to invite some of your friends over for tea. I haven't seen the Duke of Everly's daughter here for weeks. Or the Earl of Camden's daughter. Or Viscount Haversham's daughter. Or anyone else who runs in our circle."

Polly knew what her father was getting at. She knew he was making his point that Willowbrook was divided into two groups—the nobility and the commoners—and she was definitely not meant to associate with anyone who wasn't nobility.

"I did meet someone I would like to invite for tea," she said.

"Who?"

"Caroline Walters."

"Walters? That's the name of the vicar. She wouldn't be a relative of his, would she?"

"Yes, Papa," she said with a smile. "The vicar is her father."

"The vicar's daughter is not someone you should include in your circle of friends, Pauline. You are fully aware of that."

"I don't know why not, Father. She is ever so nice, and her mother died when she was barely four years old. Just like Mama did. She grew up alone, just like I did, with only her father to raise her."

"I'm sure her circumstances were nothing like ours, Pauline. I'm sure she didn't have nursemaids and governesses and a dance teacher. Or someone to teach her how to ride or the proper way to pour tea. She didn't grow up knowing how to be a proper lady like you did."

"Do you think that makes me better than her, Father?"

"It simply means that you are in a different class, Pauline. That is all."

"But Father," she started, but her father held up his hand.

"We've had this discussion before, Pauline. You know my feelings on the matter."

"Yes, Father," she replied, knowing it would do no good to argue, which would only cause him to give her another lecture on the difference between their class and commoners.

"Be sure to take Iris with you, and don't stay in town too long."

"Thank you, Papa," she said, kissing her father's cheek. "You're the best father in the world."

He smiled. "That's because I'm the only father you've ever had or known."

"You are right," she said, then reached for his hand and squeezed his fingers. "We were both pretty lucky, weren't we?" she said, then listened to his laughter as she left.

Iris walked with her, not behind her, as they headed to Willowbrook. She and Iris were friends. They'd been friends since they first met when Polly was twelve years old, and Iris had come to her as her lady's maid. Perhaps Iris was the reason Polly was able to form such close friendships with the class her father referred to as *commoners*.

"Where would you like to go first, my lady?" Iris asked.

"I want to get the ribbon I told Papa I needed…"

"Even though you have several ribbons already that match the gown you had made for yourself."

"Yes," Polly said with a smile. She hated to fool her father, but wanted to have enough time to chat with the man who owned the bookshop.

She tried to answer the question of why she was so fascinated with him. There'd been an instant attraction she couldn't explain. Not only was he ever so handsome, but his physique was totally masculine. He was as dark as Polly was light; his eyes were as deep a brown as hers were brilliant blue. And his facial features cried out for her fingers to trace them.

Polly tamped down the scandalous thought and took in a deep breath. No one had a right to be as ruggedly handsome as he was. No man should be blessed with cheekbones as high and defined as his were, or a jaw line as chiseled and unforgiving as his was. And she didn't even want to think about how muscular and well built he was.

He was what she'd once heard described as a veritable feast to the eyes. Oh, yes. He was definitely a treasure to behold. She wondered how her body would react if she had the opportunity to touch him—at least for him to take her hand.

"Here we are, my lady," Iris said as Polly nearly walked past the shop that had the largest selection of ribbons.

"Oh, I nearly missed it. I was woolgathering."

"I noticed," Iris said with a grin. "Do I want to ask what—or about whom—you were woolgathering?"

"I was just thinking about how Willowbrook has grown. We

have so many more shops than we ever had before."

"Yes, my lady. I'm sure that's exactly what you were thinking about," Iris said on a laugh.

That was the trouble with someone like Iris knowing one so well. She was quite adept at knowing when one wasn't being honest with her.

Polly turned and walked into the milliner's shop. It took her but a few minutes to select a pink ribbon she could show her father if she needed to prove that she'd actually gone shopping for one. She paid for her purchase and turned down the street in the direction of The Page Turner Bookshop.

The bell above the door rang when she entered, and the man who had lived inside her memory stood to his full height.

"Good afternoon," he greeted her with a broad smile. The wider he smiled, the deeper the creases dented either side of his mouth.

A gentle whirlpool spun deep in her stomach, and a small host of butterflies took flight.

"Good afternoon, Mr. Essex," Polly replied.

He took a few steps toward her, and she matched his footsteps until they were facing each other.

"Have you finished your books already?" he asked.

"I'm a fast reader."

"Yes, you must be. The Dumas book is quite a lengthy novel."

"Yes, but I found it so captivating I couldn't put it down."

"Oh, I'm glad you enjoyed it. Have you come to look for another book?"

"Yes. Or perhaps two."

He smiled at her, and more butterflies fluttered maddeningly. "Please, follow me. Unless you would like to choose a different genre."

"No, I noticed several books in the same area that I hadn't read yet."

"Very well," he said, then led the way to the front of the aisle, then down the next aisle. "What are you in the mood for, Lady…?"

"Lady Pauline. Lady Pauline Dearbourne."

"Lady Pauline," he repeated, and Polly felt a rush of warmth heat her chest when he said her name. His voice was deep and rich and laced with a silky smoothness that caused her flesh to tingle.

She would have preferred that he talk to her as long as he had the last time she'd been here, but just then the bell above the door jingled and two women, obviously a mother and daughter, entered, and he excused himself to assist them. Before the two women had found what they were looking for, a man entered the shop and Mr. Essex was kept busy.

Polly took her time perusing the selection of books. She knew it was wrong of her, but she procrastinated until the other customers had purchased their books and she was the last customer in line.

"Oh, my," she said as she placed two books on the counter. "You have been busy indeed. That is wonderful."

"Yes, wonderful," he said with a smile. "But a little trying, too."

Polly glanced down and saw an advertisement on the counter. "Is that why you've made this advertisement for additional help?"

"Yes. I need someone to assist me. Especially someone to work behind the counter and handle the sales."

Polly studied him for a moment. She wondered if she dared ask him for a job. "Um…" she said hesitantly.

"Yes?" he asked.

"I just wondered," she said, twisting the edge of the yellow ribbon that tied her bonnet beneath her chin. "Would you hire me if I applied for the position?"

He smiled. "I truly don't wish to insult you, but I'm afraid what I say will do exactly that."

"I'm not easily offended, sir. Please, say what you're thinking."

"Well, I don't doubt that you would make an excellent assistant. You have a love for books that is equal to mine, and you are one of the most well-read individuals I have ever had the pleasure of meeting. And," he said, broadening his smile, "you would be one of the prettiest attractions I could think of to draw customers into my store. I'm sure people would come in simply to see *you*, and not my books."

She lowered her gaze, and her cheeks heated in embarrassment. "But?"

"But you are from the nobility, my lady. Your father is of what rank?"

"Marquess."

"Of course. First of all, I doubt that he would allow you to work in a shop, just as I doubt that he would allow you to mingle with the common people who come into my shop. Am I correct?"

"Unfortunately, you are correct," she answered.

"That does not surprise me." He smiled at her and took the books she'd placed on the counter. "Oh, you must have enjoyed Alexandre Dumas. You've chosen *The Three Musketeers*. Excellent choice. And *Sense and Sensibility*. One of my favorites from Jane Austen."

"You really are unique, Mr. Essex. I didn't think I'd ever meet a man who enjoyed reading the same books that I enjoy."

He laughed. "I doubt you would enjoy some of the books I read, my lady. I also enjoy a good mystery, and some Edgar Allan Poe."

"Who is Edgar Allan Poe?"

He chuckled harder. "He is for another time, when you are a little braver and won't mind reading about talking ravens and people trapped behind walls."

"Oh my," she said with a frown. "But what kind of book is your favorite?"

He hesitated, as if he didn't want to share the kind of books he truly enjoyed. Could they be so reprehensible? Or so shocking?

"Very well," he said at last. "I will tell you if you promise not to laugh."

"I promise," she said, watching him with an excitement that was evident.

"My favorite books are children's books. Any book written for children."

"Are you serious?" she said.

"Yes, I am serious. I find the stories fascinating. They usually have a moral and teach a lesson. In fact, I've written several of my own stories."

"You write children's stories? May I see one?"

Polly saw his expression turn pensive, as if he was truly considering showing her one of his stories. Then his face fell, and she knew he'd lost the courage to share his work with her.

"I doubt you would find them interesting," he said. "Not when compared to Dumas and Austen."

"But I would love to read them. Perhaps not all of them, but at least one of them. I'll let you think about it, then I'll be back in a week and hope you've changed your mind."

He hesitated. "I'll think about it," he said.

She paid for her purchases, then walked to the door. She turned to face him before she opened the door and said, "I truly hope you will reconsider my offer and allow me to read one of your children's books. They sound fascinating."

"I'll consider it," he said, then watched her leave his shop.

Her maid met her outside and walked with her out of town.

THE WORDS HE'D spoken earlier came back to hit him in the face. They were words he needed to keep in mind when he was associating with Lady Pauline Dearbourne. He must never forget that she was beyond his reach. She was someone he could admire, but not someone he could consider in a romantic way.

Ethan watched her leave until he could no longer see her. For a long time he'd wanted to show his work to someone. He'd wanted someone to read one of the stories he'd written and give him an honest opinion of its merits. Who would be better to read one of his stories than Lady Pauline?

Whose opinion would he cherish more than hers?

CHAPTER FOUR

POLLY ENTERED THE house and found her father waiting for her in his study.

"Pauline," he said, loud enough that she had no trouble hearing him.

"Yes, Papa," she answered, handing her purchases to Iris to take to her room. When she'd removed her coat and bonnet, she went to his study. "Did you need something?" she asked, sitting in the chair before his desk.

"Yes, Pauline. I had a brilliant idea while you were out."

This was not good. Every brilliant idea her father had involved something Pauline didn't want to do.

"What is your brilliant idea, Papa?"

"Don't prepare yourself to dislike my idea before you've even heard it, dear."

"I won't, Papa."

"Yes. I can see by the look on your face and the tightness of your voice that you have."

Polly took a deep breath and tried to smile. "Very well, Papa. I'm quite excited to hear your idea."

"I knew you would be. And you will think it is an excellent idea too, once you hear it."

"I'm sure I will. Now, what is this idea of yours?"

"A grand tea."

"A grand tea?"

"Yes. We will invite all the young ladies as well as the gentlemen of our acquaintance to join us for a grand tea and dancing afterwards. I started to compose a list of the guests we should invite, but I'm sure I forgot some."

Her father's shoulders rose, and a smile lit his face. He was ever so proud of himself for having had such a brilliant idea.

She hated it.

"Well, what do you think?" he asked.

"I think it's a marvelous idea," she lied. "When were you thinking of having this event?"

"I thought perhaps next week would be ideal."

"Next week?" she squeaked. "I can't possibly organize an event this detailed in such a short time. I will need at least a month."

Polly hoped that if she could push her father's plan off by a month or two, perhaps he would forget about it. Or it would be so close to the Season, people would have left to return to London by then.

"We don't have a month, Pauline. The Season will have started by then, and I will have returned to London to meet with my committees in the House."

Lord Springdale shuffled the papers around on his desk and finally found what he was looking for. "Here, Pauline. I wanted to help you out, so I began an invitation list of all the young ladies and gentlemen I thought you would want to invite. I no doubt forgot some important people, so add whomever I missed."

Polly scanned the list of names. "Father, there are more than twenty names on this list."

"Closer to thirty, my dear."

"I can't organize a tea for thirty guests!"

"Of course you can. Iris will help you write the invitations, and I'll send several footmen out in the morning to deliver them."

"But Father—" she started, but her father held up his hand.

"What day would you like to host your tea, Pauline? Today is

Wednesday. Perhaps next Friday?"

She released a heavy sigh. "Friday would be fine."

"Good. Good," her father said excitedly. "Well, I'll let you get going on the plans. You'll have to work fast."

Polly took the list her father had drawn up and rose. She turned to leave, then stopped and turned back to face her father. "Why are you doing this, Papa?"

"Doing what, sweetheart?"

"Forcing me to host an event that I don't wish to host, and inviting a swarm of people I don't wish to entertain?"

Her father placed his pen on the desk and clenched his hands together, then lifted his head and locked his gaze with hers. "For exactly those reasons, Pauline. Because if I left you to your own devices, you would search for friends and acquaintances in the wrong places."

"And what places are those?"

"With shopkeepers and maids and stable hands and clergy-men's daughters. And you are better than that. You need to make friends from the upper class of Willowbrook. From young ladies and gentlemen in *our* class."

Polly felt a knot form in the pit of her stomach. Her father was serious, and she hated this part of him. She very much disliked the fact that he thought she was better than Caroline Waters, the vicar's daughter, or Ethan Essex, one of the most enchanting men she'd ever met.

One of the most special men she'd ever come to know.

ETHAN WAS JUST opening up in the morning when the bell above his door jingled and someone entered the shop. At first he was going to tell them that he wasn't open yet, but on second thought, he decided it might be someone who needed something special.

He walked out of the back room and looked around the shop. At first he didn't see anyone, then Lady Pauline stepped out from behind the books on the last row.

"What on earth…" he said, and rushed to where she stood. "What's wrong? Are you all right?"

She'd been crying. It was obvious. Her deep blue eyes were darker than normal, and they were rimmed in red, as was her nose.

Ethan reached out and brought her to him. He wrapped his arms around her and let her cry. When she was better, he helped her sit on a nearby low stool. Then he handed her his handkerchief and knelt on one knee in front of her. "All right, Lady Pauline. What's wrong? Are you hurt?"

She shook her head. "No, I'm just being silly and I wanted to talk to someone. I wanted to speak to you."

He smiled. "I'm flattered. That's the nicest compliment I've ever received. What would you like to talk about?"

"My father. When I returned home yesterday—"

"From here?"

She nodded.

"Was your father angry with you for coming here?"

She shook her head. "He didn't even know I'd been here."

"Then what was wrong?"

"He believes I have been associating with too many people who are *beneath us*."

"I see."

"He wanted me to host a grand tea next week, then handed me a list of all the young ladies and gentlemen I am to invite."

"All of the *titled* young ladies and gentlemen you are to invite."

"Yes. That's so unfair, Ethan. Why can't I like the friends I feel most comfortable being around?" she asked.

"Because it's important to your father that you form friendships with the people you will associate with when you return to London. He's only looking out for your own good. He wants you to have friends when you attend London's social affairs. And are not an outcast."

Lady Pauline wiped her tears then looked him in the eye. "How can you understand him so well? How do you know what he's thinking? Why aren't you as angry with him as I am?"

Ethan chuckled. "I very seldom get angry. I learned a long time ago that anger doesn't solve anything. Ever."

"Do you know how special you are?" Lady Pauline said in a breathy whisper that sent shivers down Ethan's spine.

He knew he shouldn't. He told himself he shouldn't. But he knew he was going to, even though it would be the biggest mistake of his life. He was going to kiss her. And he did.

He clasped her arms and lowered his head, then pressed his lips lightly to hers.

Their kiss wasn't long. Nor was it intense. But it was the most earth-shattering kiss he'd ever experienced. And from the look on Pauline's face, she felt the same.

He pulled away from her and stood. "Are you all right now?"

She gave three shaky nods.

"Are you ready to return home?"

She repeated her three nods.

"Stay here. I'll check outside and make sure no one sees you."

She nodded again.

Ethan walked to the door and looked down the street in both directions to make sure she wouldn't be seen leaving.

"All right," he said, and she walked up the aisle and came to him. "Don't let anyone see you. No need for some Nosey Parker to let your father know where you've been."

"I won't," she said, then grabbed his hand and kissed his fingers. "Thank you," she whispered, and turned toward the door.

He opened the door and checked in both directions again, then brushed his fingers down her cheek.

"I don't know when I'll see you again," she said.

"That's all right. You know where I'll be."

"Thank you," she said.

"Be careful."

"I will," she replied, and was gone.

Ethan watched to make certain no one saw her or followed her. Only when she was safely out of sight did he turn to go back to what he'd been doing before she arrived. Except he couldn't remember what that had been.

All he could think about was Lady Pauline, and that he'd kissed her.

He tried to tell himself that their kiss didn't mean anything, but it had. It had meant a great deal. He was attracted to her like he'd never been attracted to anyone before.

He thought of her reaction to his kiss. He wouldn't have blamed her if she had slapped him for being so forward, but she hadn't. Instead, she'd taken his hand and pressed his fingers to her lips. She'd reacted as if his kiss had been the most natural thing in the world. As if a kiss shared by them was something they'd done a thousand times before.

Oh, why had he done something so reckless? Why had he done something so dangerous? It wasn't as if he could kiss her once and that would be enough to satisfy him for the rest of his life. He'd have to kiss her over and over and over again.

POLLY STOOD AT the entrance to the room where her guests would mingle before finding their assigned seats at the four tables. Each table had one empty place. That was for her. She intended to rotate from one table to the next to meet and greet all twenty-eight guests who had been invited to her grand tea.

The room was decorated beautifully. The food Cook had prepared looked delicious. The tables were ever so inviting, and the atmosphere was delightful. Polly couldn't imagine anything more perfect.

If only Ethan could be here with her. Then she wouldn't be

so nervous. She wouldn't feel so alone.

"Everything looks lovely, Pauline. Your mother would be so proud of you."

"Thank you, Papa. Do you miss her?"

"On days such as this, more than anything."

He wrapped his arm around her shoulders as Wickers brought the first guest forward.

"Lady Phoebe and her sister Miss Amanda."

Polly greeted them as if they were long-lost friends, then turned to greet the next guests, two gentlemen, the Earl of Westing and Baron Cannoly. Within minutes, the room was filled and every seat taken.

She tried to pretend that she was enjoying every moment of her tea, but it was difficult. If only Ethan were here with her. If only he were at her side and could make this day bearable. If only he was one of the "accepted" people that her father thought fit in their circle of acquaintances. But that would never be.

Time passed ever so slowly, and finally everyone left. Polly stood at the door and bade them all farewell. When the last guest departed, she returned to the tearoom and sat in one of the empty chairs that had been designated for her and poured herself a cup of tepid tea. She'd never felt such relief in her life.

"Your affair went off without a hitch, my dear. I'm so proud of you."

"Thank you, Papa. Everyone seemed to enjoy themselves."

"Of course they did. You were the perfect hostess. I wish your mother could have seen how magnificent you re."

Polly stood on tiptoe and kissed her father's cheek.

"So, what are you going to do now?" he asked.

Polly couldn't help but frown at his question. "What do you mean?"

"Well," he said on a laugh, "I would think you would be in a hurry to go to your room and make a list of the gentlemen you met today and decide which ones you would like to have call on you again. Was there anyone who caught your eye?"

She shook her head. "No, Papa. There wasn't."

Her father reached for her hand and patted her fingers. "There's no rush, sweetheart. You have the entire Season to choose the perfect gentleman to marry. But you don't have forever, you know."

"Yes, Papa. I know."

"I wanted to tell you that tomorrow I will be going to London for a few days. I should be back the middle of next week. Is there anything you need me to bring back for you?"

"No, Papa. I don't need anything, and if I do, Willowbrook has anything I need. I can get it here."

"I won't be gone long, sweetheart. Keep Iris with you at all times."

"I will," Polly said. "Have a safe trip."

"I will. I'll see you when I get back. If the Finance Committee didn't have to meet before the next session of the House, I'd stay here and celebrate your success with you. But I can't miss this meeting. It's vitally important."

"That's all right, Papa. We can celebrate when you return."

"Yes, we'll celebrate later, darling. Good night, Pauline. Sleep well."

"I will. Good night, Papa."

Polly went to her room to think. And dream. Of the perfect man she'd already met—and couldn't have.

CHAPTER FIVE

HER FATHER WAS gone by the time she came down the next morning. Polly ate a quick breakfast, then went to the kitchen to thank Cook and the staff for the extra work they did to make her tea such a success. After she thanked everyone, she went back upstairs, gathered her cloak and bonnet, and took Iris with her on her errands.

"I hope you don't mind going out so early, Iris," she said as they followed the path that led to Willowbrook.

"Not at all, my lady," Iris replied. "I enjoy rising early. It's what I was used to doing at home. We were often up and at work before it was even light outside."

"What was your job, Iris? I assume everyone in your family had a job to do."

"Oh, yes. We each had our special tasks. There were six of us, and my two older brothers went out with Da and milked the cows, then let the animals out of the barn and took them to the fields. My older sister took care of separating the cream from the milk Da and the boys got that morning. And my mum and I started the breakfast."

"What did your two younger sisters do?"

"They were in charge of gathering the eggs and bringing them into the house."

"Do you miss the farm, Iris?" Polly asked.

"I have to admit that at times I do. But it was hard work. There wasn't anything easy about working the farm, especially during harvest and planting and putting up hay. But there were good times, too. Especially nighttime, sitting under the stars."

"I imagine those were very special times," Polly said as they entered Willowbrook.

"They were," Iris replied, then looked at Polly. "Where are we going first?"

"The bookshop, Iris."

The lady's maid laughed. "I should have known that's where you'd want to go first."

"Actually, that's the only shop I want to visit today."

"You are lucky your papa is gone. Someday he's going to realize how much time you spend at the bookshop, and he's going to forbid you from coming here."

"Don't even think that, Iris," Polly said, realizing how disastrous that would be. She didn't want to think what she'd do if her father forbade her from seeing Ethan.

Iris opened the door, and Polly went ahead of her into the bookshop. She didn't see Ethan at first until he came out of the back room with a stack of books in his arms.

"Good morning, my lady," he said, greeting her with a heart-stopping smile.

Polly's breath caught and she could hardly speak. "Good morning, Mr. Essex."

"Perhaps you would like to introduce me to your friend, and I'll direct her to some books she might find of interest."

"This is my lady's maid, Iris. She's not only my lady's maid, but we've been together so long she is also my friend."

"It's a pleasure to meet you, Iris," Ethan said with a slight bow.

"The pleasure is mine," Iris responded, "but I shall be content to browse." With that, Iris stepped away.

"So, how did your tea go?" he asked Polly as she walked along the aisle that took her to the collection of books that interested her.

"It was a success, Mr. Essex. Everyone I had invited came. There were twenty-eight guests."

"How impressive. That must mean you are highly thought of, my lady."

"Not necessarily," she countered. "It only means that there are so few social activities for society in Willowbrook that no one wanted to miss taking advantage of an opportunity to practice their social skills."

He laughed, and Polly lifted her gaze to watch him. All she could think of was the kiss they'd shared little more than a week ago. The kiss that had changed her life.

"Was your father pleased with the event?"

"Oh, more than pleased. He rained down a multitude of compliments, as if I'd accomplished the most amazing of feats."

"I'm sure you did, my lady. And you made him proud by doing such an extraordinary job."

"Well, I won't have to hear his praise for a while. He had to go to London. A meeting with the Finance Committee. Nothing prevents him from meeting with his committee. He's very devoted to the government and overseeing the committees he's on."

"Is he chairman of that committee?"

"Yes."

Ethan's expression changed. The smile left his face and his eyes narrowed with a troubled glare.

"Is something wrong, Ethan?"

"No, no. I was just thinking about something I was going to do yesterday and forgot about. But I can do it later this afternoon." He erased the worry from his face and looked at her again with a smile. "Now, have you finished reading either of the books you purchased the last time you were here?"

"Only one. I read *Sense and Sensibility*, but I've barely begun *The Three Musketeers*."

"That's because you had other things to concentrate on last

week."

"Yes, but I have decided that today I want to purchase one more book, and I want you to give me one of your children's books to read."

"Oh—" he began, but Polly held up her hand.

"I will not take no for an answer. I insist upon reading at least one of your books."

He laughed. "You are a very determined young lady."

"Oh, yes. Very. So, you may as well get one of them and give it to me. I refuse to leave until I have one to read."

"Very well," he said, then placed his hand over her fingers and gave them a gentle squeeze. "I'll be right back."

He walked to the back room, and when he returned, he had a ledger in his hands. He hesitated, then handed it to her.

Polly looked at it and smiled. Its title was *The Turtle Who Loved to Dance.* "How sweet," she said.

"And have you decided on a book for yourself?" he asked.

"I think I'd like to read something by Charles Dickens. Perhaps *David Copperfield.*"

"You'll have to let me know how you like it."

"That means you must not have liked it that much."

"No, it only means that you'll have to let me know how you liked it."

"Very well," Polly said. "I will, but first I have to finish *The Three Musketeers.*"

Just then the bell above the door jingled and two ladies entered. Ethan went to help them, and came back to her once he had them engrossed in a large volume.

"Have you found anyone to assist you in your shop?" Polly asked.

"Not as yet. But I have two applicants coming this afternoon. I haven't met them, but their references look promising. One of them was a teacher in an all-girls school, and the other was a tutor for several boys. He worked for the Earl of Waltering until his boys reached the age to go to university."

"I've heard of Lord Waltering. If he wrote your applicant references, then they will be good. Lord Waltering is a harsh but fair man, and his sons possess admirable qualities and are quite the young intellectuals."

"That speaks highly of their tutor, then. I can't wait to meet him."

"What happens if both applicants are qualified?"

Ethan smiled. "I will hire them both. It's important to have one person to assist the customers, and one to take care of the money."

"Then what are you going to do?"

He laughed. "I'm going to steal you away to the back room and show you all the new books that have arrived."

"You are terrible, Mr. Essex."

"I know I am, but I can't help it. You bring out the worst in me."

"I will have to change you, then, so I only bring out your best."

The bell above the door rang again, and Polly stepped back from Ethan. She hadn't realized she'd moved so close to him. She didn't remember moving, but she must have.

She glanced toward the door and stepped back further. It was Lady Franken, one of the most worrisome wags in Willowbrook. When it came to gossip, none could outdo the good lady. Polly noticed that Iris had risen from her chair and taken several steps toward her.

"I must be going. I've been away far too long already." Polly walked to the counter to pay for her book.

"Will I see you tomorrow?" Ethan asked quietly.

"Only if you wish to," she answered, raising her chin to meet his eyes.

"It would be my fondest hope."

His smile set her cheeks ablaze.

"Thank you, Mr. Essex," she murmured, then walked to the door. "Good day, Lady Franken. Have you come in search of a book?"

"Yes, I have. Do you have any suggestions, Lady Pauline?"

"Have you read Jane Austen?"

"Not as yet. Do you recommend her?"

"Most heartily," Polly said. "I would suggest either *Pride and Prejudice* or *Sense and Sensibility*. I enjoyed both of them most thoroughly."

"Well, thank you for your suggestions, my lady. They were most helpful."

"You are welcome, my lady. Good day," Polly said with a nod, then walked out the door Iris held open for her.

When they stepped outside and the door closed behind them, Iris reached to carry Polly's package. "That was a near disaster, my lady. I only hope she wasn't aware of how long you were in the bookshop. That will cause her tongue to wag."

"I know, Iris. Let's go to the tea shop and get a cup of tea. I'll even treat you to a pastry."

"That sounds delightful, my lady."

The two walked down the street until they reached the tea shop. Polly thought about what Iris had said. She was right to warn her. The last thing she needed was for her father to hear rumors of her spending an excessive amount of time in the bookshop.

THE MINUTE POLLY got home, she took the book she'd purchased and the manuscript of Ethan's children's book up to her room. She made herself comfortable in the window seat and read his pages. It was enchanting—a delightful story with a message, teaching children the necessity of being polite and thinking of others before one's self.

The spotted turtle named Tommy was the best dancer in the forest, and every time the animals had a celebration, he was the animal most in demand to partner the other animals.

Sally, the sly fox, believed herself to be the prettiest animal at the dance and was the first to come to Tommy to ask him to dance with her. Polly chuckled at how closely that mirrored real life.

And there were Russell Rabbit and Fanny Fawn and Gus Gazelle. They were all very talented dancers and expected Tommy to want to dance with them because they were so light on their paws.

But Tommy Turtle wasn't happy just dancing with the animals that were the best dancers and the most popular animals in the forest. He wanted to dance with everyone—especially the animals that no one liked. Like Sidney Skunk, because sometimes he didn't smell so good. And Penelope Porcupine, because sometimes she left stickers in her partners' paws. And Susie Sloth, because she moved so slowly she had a difficult time keeping up with the music.

But Tommy didn't care. He wanted to dance with everyone. Especially the animals who sometimes weren't asked to dance at all. And he wanted every animal there to enjoy themselves.

When the dance was over and everyone went home to their dens or nests, or burrows, or wherever they lived, he wanted them to have enjoyed the celebration. He wanted each of them to go to sleep with smiles on their faces and have pleasant dreams all night long.

So what did you learn from Tommy? the last line in the book asked.

Answers:

1. *No animal is better than another animal, just like no person is better than another person.*

2. *It is more important that everyone enjoys themselves rather than just a few.*

3. *Each one of us has the power to make every experience positive for all.*

The moment Polly turned the last page of Ethan's manuscript, she jumped from her chair and took out her paper and paints. She'd always loved drawing and painting, and she couldn't help but imagine how much more vivid the story would be if there were illustrations that went along with the words.

She started with a picture of Tommy Turtle dancing and twirling across the page. And then she sketched the second drawing. And the third. And the fourth...

CHAPTER SIX

"**A**RE YOU STILL working?" Iris asked as she brought in a tray and set it on the corner of the desk. "May I see what you're drawing?"

Polly hesitated. These drawings were special. She felt as though they were meant to be shared with Ethan first, before the rest of the world could see them.

Then she realized how foolish that was. These were simply drawings. The same as she'd done a thousand times before.

Polly picked them up and held them out for Iris to take.

She watched Iris's expression change as she turned over each drawing. At first her gaze was quizzical, but gradually the girl's smile grew brighter with each new character she met.

"Oh, my lady," she exclaimed. "Are these what I think they are?"

"They're illustrations for—"

"Yes! For the book Mr. Essex gave you! These are precious, my lady. Adorable. I love them!"

"Do you really?"

"Oh, I do. I love Tommy Turtle. He must be the hero. The very image of the man we all dream about. Oh!" Iris giggled, putting her hand over her mouth. "Imagine me thinking about a turtle being my hero."

Polly smiled at the idea.

"And look at the way you gave each character such personality. They are adorable. Each one of them are so precious you want to pick them up and squeeze them. Even Penelope Porcupine and Susie Sloth. They are ever so cute."

"Do you think so?"

"Oh, I do. When are you going to show them to Mr. Essex?"

"Not until they're all completed. Hopefully I can have them finished by tomorrow afternoon. We will see."

"Remember to eat your dinner so you don't starve," Iris scolded. "You haven't had anything to eat since our tea and pastry this morning. I'll be back after you've eaten and help you get ready for bed."

"Thank you, Iris," Polly said as the lady's maid walked to the door.

"You like him, don't you?" Iris asked, pausing with her hand on the doorknob.

"Who?" Polly asked, trying to sound innocent.

"You know who I mean," Iris said with a smile.

Polly breathed a heavy sigh. "Yes, I like him," she admitted.

"You know you can never be more than friends, though, don't you?"

"I know, Iris."

"Perhaps it would be better if you didn't let yourself have feelings for him, my lady. Your father will never allow you to associate with him. No matter how close you become. It will only cause problems."

Polly watched the door close behind Iris and knew everything she'd said was correct. Allowing herself to have feelings for Ethan would only cause heartache. In the end, she'd have to choose between her father and Ethan.

She poured herself a cup of tea and took a sip. She wasn't hungry enough to stop her work on Ethan's book, so she picked at her food while she continued to draw. She wanted to have at least some of the sketch completed before she went to sleep. She wanted Ethan to see what she'd drawn and if he thought they enhanced his book.

But most of all, she simply wanted to see him again.

➤➤➤✦◀◀◀

ETHAN HAD CONTACTED the two candidates who applied to be his assistants. He met with them briefly and hired both of them on the spot. They were each more than qualified and would complement each other perfectly.

But most of all, he needed to decide what he would do about the job the queen had given him.

He had done some investigating the night before and verified that Lady Pauline's father was indeed the Marquess of Springdale. He was, without a doubt, the man Ethan was supposed to eliminate. But how could he? He'd lose her forever if she discovered what he intended to do.

Hell, he'd lose her forever if she discovered what he was. How could she ever want anything to do with a man who was a hired assassin?

But what were his choices?

Perhaps he could go to the queen and tell her he couldn't kill the Marquess of Springdale. But that wouldn't make everything right. The queen would only assign someone else to assassinate the marquess.

The fact that she'd raised some doubts as to his guilt told Ethan that he had to discover beyond any doubt that Lady Pauline's father was guilty of embezzling money from the Finance Committee he oversaw. But how could he do that? The only way he thought possible was to get inside Springdale's country manor and look at the marquess's ledgers. And if the queen's suspicions were correct, he would also find correspondence with foreign agents. Finding some evidence detailing his transactions was the surest way of assessing Springdale's guilt or innocence.

He considered what he had to do and plotted the best way to accomplish it. He'd thought Lady Pauline would come this morning, but she hadn't—which meant she would hopefully come this afternoon. Perhaps he would have time to speak with her in private. Mr. Tumberly and Mrs. Tenpin were to come in at one o'clock and work a half-day until five. That would give Ethan a little while to oversee his new employees, then spend some uninterrupted time with the young woman he found so captivating.

The bell above the door jingled, and Mr. Tumberly and Mrs. Tenpin arrived at the same time.

"Good afternoon," he greeted them. He shook Tumberly's hand and nodded to Mrs. Tenpin.

"Good afternoon," they chimed.

"Hopefully, we'll be busy enough this afternoon that you'll get an idea of how the bookshop runs. When you're not busy, I suggest you walk around the shop and memorize how the books are arranged. It's extremely important that when a customer comes in with a request for a certain book, or the topic of books he wants to peruse, that you know where to take him. That will give the customers confidence in your abilities."

Just then, the bell above the door jingled again and a couple entered the bookshop looking for any books Ethan might have on farming practices in the modern age. He led them to the correct area and indicated which books might be the most helpful for them.

The bell jingled a second time, and an elderly gentleman entered. He asked if they had any books on Crimea and the war that had recently ended there.

A little while later, two young ladies entered wanting to see the stationery The Page Turner Bookshop carried. Without hesitation, Mrs. Tenpin stepped up to help them. While she led them to the stationery section, Mr. Tumberly went to the register and made change for the man who'd purchased two books on farming practices.

Ethan was more than pleased with the two candidates he'd hired. He had no doubt that they would be able to be left alone before long.

The next time the bell jingled, Lady Pauline entered the shop.

Ethan held up his hand to indicate that Mrs. Tenpin and Mr. Tumberly didn't need to assist the lady. He walked to her and extended his arm for her to take, then led her to meet his new assistants.

"Lady Pauline, allow me to introduce Mrs. Tenpin, my new associate, and Mr. Tumberly, my new assistant."

"How do you do?" Lady Pauline said, and Mrs. Tenpin curtsied politely as Mr. Tumberly bowed.

"Lady Pauline is a special client of mine, and we have some business to discuss," Ethan said. "We'll be close by in the back room, so if you have any questions, or need any assistance, please come get me. I'll be at your disposal."

"Yes, Mr. Essex," they said, and Ethan escorted Lady Pauline to the area of the back room he'd set aside as his office.

Iris followed them, and he arranged a chair near an empty table where she could work on an embroidery project she'd brought along. "Please, have a seat, my lady," he said.

When they were both settled, Lady Pauline looked at him and smiled. "I'm impressed with them," she said. "They seem very congenial."

"They are. I can't believe how fortunate I was to have found them. They've only been here half a day, and as you see, I can already leave them alone for a short while."

"Oh, I'm so pleased, Ethan. This will give you the opportunity to work on your accounts and your children's books while they take care of the shop."

He felt an unexpected nervous turmoil in his mid-chest.

"Are you saying you enjoyed my book? Or it needs more work?"

"I'm saying you should write more just like it because it is fabulous," she replied.

"You really think so?"

"I know so. Your story is charming. Children are going to love it."

Ethan laid a hand on his chest, surprised at the relief he felt, and astonished at how important her opinion was to him.

"You certainly know how to build a man's ego."

Her eyebrows knitted above her lips that opened prettily in amusement.

"You really don't know how wonderful your story is, do you?"

"Well, I know it's an average story, and some children will enjoy it. But some children may not," Ethan said.

"As it is with every book ever written. Even Jane Austen. Some readers love her work, and some readers don't see the magnificence in it. The only thing I would change is—"

"Wait, let me get a paper and pen. I want to take notes."

"You won't need a paper and pen. I brought my suggestions with me."

"You did?"

"Yes. Would you like to see them?"

"Of course."

"Very well," Lady Pauline said, then took his manuscript out of the tapestry bag she carried and placed it on the table. She turned it around so it faced Ethan and opened it.

"What is this?" he asked.

"These are illustrations that go with your story. They aren't finished. I want to add more, but you'll get the idea."

"You painted these?"

"Yes."

Ethan was stunned. What lay before him was a collection of the most charming caricatures one could imagine. They were sweet, lively, engaging—the very things a child could love.

"They are fantastic, my lady."

She laid a delicate gloved hand over his. "Please, you must call me Polly. And no, it's your characters that are fantastic. I merely painted what you described. Here's Tommy Turtle. And here's Russell Rabbit, and Gus Gazelle. Oh," she said, turning another page. "Here's Penelope Porcupine, and Susie Sloth, and… Well, you get the idea."

"These are remarkable, Lady…, um, Polly." He looked up from the page to see her reaction to his informal use of her name, and the pleasure on her face warmed him. "Where did you learn to draw like this?"

"All Society females learn to draw and paint and play the piano and dance. My father insisted on only the very best tutors, you see. I don't have many talents, but drawing is one of my favorite pastimes. Drawing and reading."

"These add so much to my story. They make the characters come alive. I can't thank you enough."

"Just remember, I'm not finished. I have to touch them up yet, and there are a few animals I haven't drawn. I'll take the manuscript home with me and finish, then bring it back to you."

Ethan couldn't stop himself. He had to touch her. He wanted to kiss her, but her lady's maid sat just a few yards away. Iris had her back to them, but would no doubt realize what they were doing. So he simply reached out his hand and held hers.

"How long will your father be gone?" he whispered.

"A few more days."

"Tell me how to get into your garden. I want to see you tonight."

"Yes."

Polly whispered to him where to get in through an opening in the hedgerow, then which paths to follow to reach the terrace unseen. She promised she'd have the French doors that opened to the library unlocked for him.

"I should return home now," she said brightly. "I want to finish these."

Ethan helped her to her feet without letting go of her hand.

"Do you have a way to get your book published?" she asked.

"I don't know. There are a few publishers in London who

cater to children's books. If I'm lucky, perhaps one of them will want to publish it."

"I'm sure once they read your story, they'll want to be a part of your success."

Ethan couldn't help but smile at her enthusiasm. He knew she was about to leave, but he couldn't let her go until he kissed her at least once. He lowered his head and pressed his lips to hers.

Their kiss was the briefest he could manage while Iris collected her things just beyond them. But it wasn't enough. He needed to show Polly how desperate he was to love her. He wanted her to know how much he cared for her. He wanted her to know how special she was, even though the voice in the back of his mind was telling him that he was getting in too deep. Nothing good could come of this.

He pressed a second kiss, but she raised her hands and cupped his cheeks. "I have to go," she whispered.

"Yes. I'll see you tonight," he said, then kissed her palm.

She blushed as she turned away from him.

He could scarcely wait until nightfall.

ETHAN LOCKED THE door to his bookshop, then walked the long way to Springdale Hall. He had a lot of thinking to do. He needed to figure out what he was going to do.

Ever since he'd kissed Lady Pauline, he'd known he was going down the wrong road. He was a commoner, and she was nobility. He was Her Majesty's number one assassin. He killed people for a living. Granted, his targets were bad people who threatened Britain and her democracy, but he killed them. And worst of all, he was supposed to kill her father. It was sheer folly to think he could murder her father and think they had a chance of a life together. She could never love him. All she'd ever feel for him would be loathing and hatred.

No, he had to end his relationship with Polly tonight. And he had to make it final. He had to convince her that he didn't love her, and he never would. And when he finished, he had to make sure she hated him.

Ethan stopped along the path and leaned back against a large oak tree to think. He wasn't sure he could do it. He wasn't sure he could intentionally hurt her like he knew his words would hurt her. But he didn't have a choice.

Of course, he would make sure that Polly's father was guilty of the crimes the queen had accused him of, but then he would have no choice but to follow the queen's orders. He'd have no choice but to eliminate the Marquess of Springdale.

Ethan pushed himself away from the tree and made his way to Springdale Hall, even though his heart was breaking.

Even though he wasn't sure he could survive the remainder of his life without her.

CHAPTER SEVEN

E THAN FOLLOWED POLLY'S instructions and found the hidden gate in the hedgerow. It was unlocked, and he pushed it open and entered the garden. He followed the path Polly had described and walked up the three steps to the terrace. He crossed the terrace and opened the set of multi-paned French doors and found himself in the library. He saw her right away, and watched as she ran across the room and into his arms.

Ethan gathered her close and pressed his mouth to hers. For one last time, he wanted her like he'd never wanted anyone before. Needed her like he'd never needed anyone in his life.

One last time.

He deepened his kisses and demanded more from her.

She answered his entreaties by skimming her hands up his chest and wrapping her arms around his neck. Her fingers moved across his jaw and raked through his hair.

He wanted her with an intensity that caused his blood to boil. His breathing became harsh and heavy, revealing his rising passion. He stole the air from her lungs until she gasped.

He kissed her again, and she answered with a series of moans that weakened his knees. She moaned again, and this time he broke off their kiss while she could still breathe.

"Polly," he gasped. He wrapped his arms around her and held her one last time. "I'm sorry I was so demanding. Are you all right?"

She stood with a trembling hand covering her quivering lips. "I don't know," she answered. "I've never felt like this."

He forced himself to chuckle, although that was the last thing he wanted to do. The last thing she would expect.

"What is so humorous?"

Nothing. Not one blasted thing.

With immense effort Ethan forced all emotion from his face.

"Oh, nothing. Just how easy it is to please you."

"What are we…going to do?"

"About what?" he asked.

"About the way we feel for each other. What are we going to do?"

"We're going to do the only thing we can."

"What is that?"

Ethan led her to a sofa and sat down beside her. He wrapped his arm around her shoulders and nestled her close to him. "We're going to stop this before it goes any further."

"No," she cried out.

"We have to, Polly," he insisted, hoping he sounded reasonably casual.

"No, Ethan. I can't," she said with a heavy voice.

"We have to," he repeated. "We've always known nothing could come from this little distraction."

"Distraction?"

"Of course. How would your father react if he discovered us here, like this?"

"Oh, Ethan."

"We don't belong together, Polly. I'm Mr. Ethan Essex. Commoner. Shopkeeper. I'm not in your class. And you are Lady Pauline Dearbourne, daughter of the Marquess of Springdale. If your father found out we were meeting like this and that I'd kissed you, he'd call me out. This can't happen again, Polly. I don't want to fight your father. I don't want to kill him."

"You'd kill my father?"

"If he were going to kill me. I'd have to."

"I can't believe you would do that."

"Well, believe it, Polly. I killed many men during the war. I'm used to killing."

"Don't say that, Ethan. You would never kill my father."

"You'd rather he killed me?"

"No! I can't give you up either. I just found you."

"And now you'll have to give me up," he said. His heart was breaking, but he couldn't let up. He had to make sure she hated him when he finished.

"I can't," she said.

He knew she was crying, but he had to stop what they were doing before it was too late. This was hopeless. "Yes, you can. We'll see each other when you come into the bookshop, but that will be it. You'll go to London in a month or so and meet several men you'll like as well as you think you like me."

"No, I won't, Ethan."

"Yes, you will," he said with as much anger in his voice as he could summon. "You are just reading too much into your feelings."

"But I love you."

Ethan shook his head. "You can't, Polly. I don't love you!"

"What did you say?"

"I said you can't love me because I don't love you."

The second he said those words, he wanted to take them back. But it was too late. He had to make her believe there was no hope for them. He had to make her believe he didn't love her. No matter how much it hurt her.

No matter how much it hurt him.

"How could you let me believe you did?" she said through her tears.

A sharp pain centered in his chest. He had to let her go. Every time he kissed her, their kisses were more intense. They were more demanding. Eventually he wouldn't be able to stop with just kissing her. He'd give in and make love to her, as he already had a dozen times in his craven mind. He had to stop their feelings for each other before it was too late. And he had to make it clear to her that there was no hope for them.

He knew his words had hurt her, but he didn't have a choice. He had to convince her that he didn't love her. That he couldn't love anyone. That he had his entire future ahead of him and wasn't about to let an emotion he didn't even believe in destroy what he wanted to do with his life.

"The love you think you feel for me will go away, Polly."

"What if it doesn't? How will I be able to go on when you possess my heart?"

Ethan forced himself to laugh. "I don't possess your heart, Polly. You are just imagining it. It's a schoolgirl fantasy."

"Is that what you think my feelings are? Schoolgirl fantasies?"

"What else can they be, Polly? You're not old enough to have real feelings for me. You're only, what? Twenty-two? Twenty-three? And I'm nine and twenty."

Her body went stiff in his arms, and she pulled away from him. "Is this what you truly think of me? That I am so immature that I don't know what love is?"

"How many times have you been in love, Polly? Is this your first time? You can't recognize true love. You're not experienced enough."

Polly got to her feet. "I think you need to leave, Ethan."

"Yes. I think it's time."

Ethan rose and walked to the French doors that led onto the terrace.

"I loved you, Ethan. Don't ever try to tell me I'm not old enough or experienced enough to know what love feels like. Because I did. Until you killed it."

Ethan didn't answer her. He knew he couldn't convince her that she wasn't old enough or experienced enough to realize that the emotions she felt for him weren't love. Because they were.

Just as he couldn't convince himself that he didn't love her. Because it was too late. He already did.

POLLY LAID AWAKE all night. She couldn't sleep. She didn't think she'd ever sleep again. Nor did she think she would ever stop crying. She'd skipped two Seasons already. This was going to be her third, and she knew she'd never find anyone she could love like she loved Ethan.

But how could she think that she loved him when he didn't love her?

Polly knew she wasn't about to go to sleep, and rather than lie awake in bed all night, she rose and put on her robe, then sat down at her desk with Ethan's book in front of her. She hadn't finished all the drawings she wanted to do, or touched up the drawings she'd already made.

Why she even wanted to work on them anymore was a mystery to her. She wasn't even sure Ethan liked them. If he could lie so easily to her and make her believe that he loved her, what made her think she could believe him when he told her that he loved her drawings? He probably hated them but hadn't decided to tell her yet.

Polly took out her paints and finished one picture, then another, until they were nearly all finished and the sun had come up in the sky.

"What are you doing up?" Iris asked, coming into the room with a tea tray and a cup of hot chocolate. "Or haven't you even been to bed yet?"

Polly put down her brushes and looked up at Iris. She didn't even have time to focus on her friend before her eyes filled with tears and the first of the heavy, wet drops streamed down her cheeks.

"What's wrong, my lady?" Iris asked, wrapping her arms around Polly and pulling her close.

Polly was sobbing so hard she couldn't explain what had happened. She was too embarrassed to tell Iris how naïve and immature she had been to allow herself to believe that Ethan had loved her when he hadn't.

"What did he do?" Iris asked.

"How do you know it was something Ethan did?"

"Because no female cries this hard over anything except something a man does. So, what was it?"

Polly took the handkerchief Iris handed her and dried her eyes, then explained what had happened.

"And you believed him?"

"Of course I believed him. You would have too if you had heard him, Iris. He was almost laughing at me for being such a fool."

"Then he's a mighty fine actor, my lady."

Polly shook her head. "You didn't see him, Iris. Or hear him."

"You're right, my lady. But I've seen him with you all these weeks, and I know what I saw. He loves you. If he told you he doesn't, he's lying."

Polly couldn't believe Iris. She wanted to, but she couldn't. She'd been fooled by him once. She refused to allow him to make a fool of her again.

Polly picked up her brushes and dipped them into the blue paint.

"Are you working on Mr. Essex's book?" Iris asked.

"Yes," Polly answered. "I can't abide leaving a project half-finished. And his work is extremely good. Children will love reading his story, and it will mean much more to them if they can actually see the characters."

"Why don't you rest for a bit, and I'll bring you up a pastry and a pot of hot water?"

"Perhaps I'll lie down for a little while, then work on my drawings later. It will take me a few more days to finish, then you can give them to Ethan for me and I can concentrate on forgetting him."

ETHAN CREPT THROUGH the gate hidden in the hedgerow, and made his way to the terrace, then to the French doors. They were locked, but this wasn't the first time he'd had to break into a locked room. In his line of work, he was an expert at it.

He doubted anything was hidden in the library. More than likely, the marquess kept his ledgers in his study, where he could update them whenever he had another deposit to add to his growing stash of stolen money.

Ethan knew he didn't have much time. He could only spend a few minutes searching before he needed to leave. And he didn't know how many days he had before Polly's father returned from London.

He entered several rooms before he found the one he assumed was Lord Springdale's study. In the center of the room was an oversized desk whose desktop was immaculately clean. Not a pencil or pen was out of place. Not a paper was strewn about. Everything was neat and tidy and put away.

Ethan was glad. This would be a simple search because immaculate people kept good records, and it would be easier to find what he was looking for.

He was just about to search for the marquess's ledgers when two maids walked past the study. From the sound of it, they were from the kitchen and were discussing why Cook had ordered them to get up at the same time as usual when the master wasn't home and Lady Pauline had touched hardly any food for more than a day.

Ethan stopped what he was doing and absorbed their words. He knew why Polly wasn't eating. It was because of the terrible things he'd said to her. It was because of the lies he'd told her. It was because he'd broken her heart.

What if she became ill? What if she didn't eat enough to sustain herself? What if—

More servants walked past the study, and Ethan rose and left the room. He couldn't risk staying here any longer. If he did, he'd eventually be discovered.

There were two multi-paned French doors that led from the study to the terrace beyond, and he followed the path that took him to the gate hidden in the hedgerow. He exited Lord Springdale's garden and made his way back to The Page Turner Bookshop.

He couldn't stop thinking about Polly. What if she truly was ill? If she were, it would be his fault. He'd be responsible for whatever happened to her. And he could never forgive himself.

CHAPTER EIGHT

Ethan had gone back to Springdale Hall the past two nights to go through the man's ledgers. He hadn't found anything that linked him to the amount of money that was missing from the Finance Committee, and only hoped that this meant the marquess was innocent. Last night he'd discovered a safe hidden in the wall behind several books, but he couldn't guess the code that unlocked it. He'd try again tonight.

"Is there anything special you'd like us to do today when we're not busy?" Mrs. Tenpin asked.

Ethan broke out in a sincere smile. He couldn't believe how fortunate he was to have two such remarkable people working for him. They were absolutely fantastic employees.

"Actually, there is. This shipment of books came in late last night, and I didn't get them catalogued and shelved. I'll let you do that."

"Of course," Mr. Tumberly and Mrs. Tenpin said together.

Ethan got out the record book where he catalogued his books and placed it on the counter. He meticulously explained how he cataloged the new arrivals so all the information was written down in case he needed to reorder any of the books. Then he wrote down the price for each book and handed them the sheet that had the prices on it.

Just as he finished explaining his procedure, the bell above the door jingled and he looked up.

"I'll take care of this customer," he said, watching as Polly's lady's maid, Iris, entered his shop. "Good day, Iris. How are you?"

"I'm fine, Mr. Essex."

"And how is your mistress?"

"She's feeling poorly," Iris said.

Ethan closed his eyes for a second and breathed a heavy sigh.

"I know there's a reason you said those horrible lies, Mr. Essex, but the day will come when you will regret them," she said.

"I already do, Iris. But I had no choice."

"Don't you think she deserves an explanation?"

"She does," he admitted. "But I'm not at liberty to give her one."

"That's not going to mean much to her when she lives a life of misery and loneliness. But hopefully she will realize that your life is no better or happier than hers."

Ethan felt as if Iris had stabbed him through the heart. Every word she said was true. He didn't stand a chance of finding another woman he could love even half as much as he loved Polly. And he couldn't imagine marrying someone he didn't love. He'd be miserable.

"Does she need something? Is there a reason you're here?"

Iris reached into the bag she carried and took out his book. She handed it to him and stepped back.

"She finished your drawings. She said your book was too good not to get it published, that children needed to read it and enjoy it."

Ethan looked at the drawings she'd added to her original set. They were magnificent. As good as the others.

He held the book with Polly's drawings to his chest. "Tell your mistress thank you," he said.

"You could always call on her yourself and thank her."

Ethan shook his head. "That would be like rubbing salt in a wound."

"Yes, it most likely would," she replied, and then the lady's maid turned around and left.

Ethan felt hollow and empty. He realized Iris was his only connection to the woman he loved, and even that connection was being severed.

⤞⤝

ETHAN WENT THROUGH the gate in the hedgerow then across the terrace and unlocked the French doors that opened into the Marquess of Springdale's study. He went immediately to the safe that was hidden in the wall behind the books. He'd come a little earlier tonight because he was determined that he would figure out the combination to the safe and see what was in it.

He'd only been working on the combination a few minutes when the door opened and Polly stepped into the room.

Ethan spun away from the safe.

"Would you like to tell me what you're doing, Mr. Essex?"

Polly's face was pale. Her eyes were open wide. And in one hand she held a candle, while in the other she clutched a pistol.

"Would you like to put down that pistol first, my lady?" he asked. The weapon was cocked and aimed at his chest.

"What I'd like to do is fire this pistol and see how fast you bleed all over this expensive rug. And if I'm not satisfied with how fast you bleed out, I might pull the trigger a second time and make the bullet hole twice as big."

Ethan slowly raised his hands in surrender. "You would shoot an unarmed man?" he asked.

"If that man was you? Yes."

"I deserved that," he said, hoping she might hear it as an apology.

"Oh, you deserve far more than that, Ethan. And, as hurt and angry as I am with you, I might find a way to make you suffer."

"I know, Polly," he said.

"Stop calling me that."

"What?"

"My nickname. Only people I consider friends are allowed to use that name."

"What would you like me to call you, then?"

"I would like for you not to call me anything. In fact, I prefer that you don't talk to me."

"Might I convince you to put that gun down before it goes off?"

She looked at him with a hostile yet defeated look then lowered her gun. "What are you doing here, Ethan? And don't lie to me. I'm tired of your lies."

"Would you mind if I pour us something to drink?"

When she didn't answer him, he assumed she didn't mind. He walked to her father's liquor table and poured them each a glass. He poured whisky for himself and wine for her, then walked to where she stood.

"Please, sit down," he said, making sure he didn't use her name.

When she sat, he handed her the glass of wine and took his whisky to the chair opposite her.

"Start talking," she said after she'd taken a sip of her wine. "Did you come to steal from my father? Are you a thief?"

"No. I'm an assassin."

She was in the process of taking another sip, and his statement shocked her so intensely that she sputtered her mouthful of wine then coughed until she almost choked.

Ethan took the glass from her hands, then gave her his handkerchief. When she finally caught her breath and stopped coughing, he gave her back her glass.

"Take a swallow."

She did, then glared at him. "That wasn't funny."

"It wasn't intended to be."

"You are an assassin? You kill people?"

"I work for the queen."

"Queen Victoria? *Our* queen?"

"Yes, our queen."

"What are you doing here? Are you working for the queen now?"

"Yes, and I'm gathering evidence."

"What kind of evidence?"

Ethan stopped long enough to take Polly's glass to the liquor table and refill it. He gave it back to her, and while she reached for it, he leaned down and snatched the pistol from beside her on the sofa and placed it out of her reach.

"Are you going to assassinate me?" she asked.

Ethan rolled his eyes. "No, I'm not going to assassinate you. I just want to make sure you don't assassinate *me.*"

"Are you going to tell me something that will make me *want* to assassinate you?"

"Yes."

"What? Does it have something to do with my father?"

"Yes."

She shifted on the sofa, and Ethan could tell by the furrows on her forehead and the angry look on her face that she was going to argue with him before he said his first word.

"Calm down, Polly."

"I told you not to call me that."

"I'm sorry."

He waited until she didn't seem quite as angry, then waited a little while longer. "Tell me when you're ready to hear what I have to say."

She took in a big breath, then another sip of wine. "Very well. Start from the beginning, and don't leave anything out."

"When I enlisted in Her Majesty's Army, I earned a reputation for being an excellent shot. It didn't take my commanding officers long to discover I had a talent for hitting whatever I aimed at. Whenever the army needed someone eliminated in a...clandestine way, they called on me. I resigned when the war was over, but Her Majesty refused to accept my resignation. She would only let me out if I agreed to help her when our country was in special trouble."

"Did you have to…eliminate someone often?"

"Often enough. But I was paid well, which allowed me to start my bookshop. Most shop owners will have to work half their lives to pay off their loans. I am almost out of debt already. The bookshop will be debt-free in a year's time."

"How does this involve my father?"

"Soon after I purchased my shop, Her Majesty asked to see me. She told me she had another assignment for me. I told her I would do this one last assignment, but then I was finished. I wouldn't do any more killing."

"Do you enjoy killing, Ethan?"

He bolted from his seat. "Hell no! I hate it. But the men I am ordered to kill aren't good men, Polly. They're our country's enemies. Most of them are traitors, if not worse. Most of them have sold military secrets to our enemies, or stolen classified information that the government doesn't want the world to see. Three of them plotted to kill the queen and the prime minister. Had that happened, our government would have been lucky to survive the upheaval. Most likely it would have collapsed, and life as we know it in England would forever be changed."

"Why don't you just arrest them and try them in a court of law?" she asked.

"Because the government doesn't want their crimes to become public. It would cause more chaos if the public were to find out what the killers had planned and how close they came to executing their plans."

"So how is my father involved in this?"

"Her Majesty received a report that nearly one hundred thousand pounds has been stolen from the Finance Committee."

A frown deepened across Polly's brow. "That's the committee my father chairs."

"Yes." Ethan could tell the second her brain connected the theft to her father's involvement in it.

"Surely you don't think Father had anything to do with the theft!"

"That's what I need to figure out. Her Majesty is convinced your father is responsible."

"No! Father would never steal anything. You know he wouldn't, Ethan."

"That's just it, Polly. I don't know. I've never even met your father. I don't know what he's capable of."

Tears formed in Polly's eyes and spilled over her lashes. "He wouldn't, Ethan. Father would never steal anything. He's not a thief."

"I hope not, Polly."

She wiped the tears from her eyes. "What were you doing here?"

"I was trying to open this safe."

"What were you hoping to find?"

"I was hoping to find a ledger that would prove your father hadn't taken any money."

"Or you were hoping to be able to prove that he had."

Ethan couldn't answer her. That was exactly what he was hoping to prove. He just wanted to know one way or the other whether her father was guilty.

"Then what were you supposed to do?" she asked.

"Her Majesty doesn't want to ruin your father's name. That would not only destroy him, but it would destroy you, too."

"You were going to kill him, weren't you?"

"I wouldn't have a choice."

"You could let him go. You could let him go to France or the Americas."

"If I didn't complete my assignment, someone else would. If your father stole from the government, he'd have to pay, Polly. You know that."

"No!" she cried, then rose to her feet and paced the room.

Ethan let her go back and forth several times without trying to stop her. Finally, it was she who stopped in front of him.

"I have to prove Father didn't steal that money."

"Are you sure he didn't, Polly?"

"Of course I'm sure. Father is the most honest man you will ever meet. He'd never steal from his country. He'd never do anything that would tarnish the Springdale title. Never!"

Tears welled in her eyes again and streamed down her cheeks. Ethan couldn't stand to see her cry. He got to his feet and went to her, wrapped his arms around her, and brought her close to him. He was surprised that she allowed him to hold her, but he was glad she did. He ached for her. It hurt him as much as it did her to think her father might have done something so terrible.

"It's all right, Polly. I'm here. I'll help you. If your father is innocent, we'll find the proof we need."

Ethan held her several minutes longer. He loved her. He'd loved her for a long time now but couldn't tell her. He didn't know how this was going to turn out. He couldn't make her any promises. Not until he knew if Lord Springdale was guilty or innocent.

A long while later, Polly lifted her head and looked at him. "If you don't find anything in the ledgers, will it prove Father didn't take the money?"

"Not exactly. He could have hidden it somewhere else."

"And if you do find a large sum of money?"

Ethan breathed a heavy sigh. "Let's worry about that when we get there."

"But it won't be good, will it?"

He didn't want to answer her. It would only make things worse. "Do you know where your father keeps the combination to his safe?"

Polly walked to the safe, turned the dial several times, then opened it.

"Your father gave you the combination?"

"Yes. He wanted someone to be able to open it if something ever happened to him, but he didn't want to write it down where someone could find it."

"That was intelligent of him."

"He thought it was, but I asked him what would happen if we both died in the same accident."

Ethan smiled. "What did he say?"

"He said not to worry. One other person had the combination in case that happened."

"Did he tell you who?"

She shook her head. "It must have been someone he trusted, though. Father wouldn't have given it to just anyone."

Ethan nodded, then stepped in front of Polly and lifted out the contents of the safe. Several of the items only held personal significance: her mother's engagement ring, which Polly told him had been passed down from her father's mother and her mother before that. A beautiful drawing of Polly's mother and father on their wedding day, which brought fresh tears to Polly's eyes. Several papers, including a copy of her father's last will and testament, which Ethan didn't need to read, and told Polly she didn't want to read either. And finally, the ledger that he'd been searching for.

"Is this what you need?" she asked.

"Yes," he said, placing everything else back in the safe before closing the door and locking it.

Ethan carried the ledger to Lord Springdale's desk and opened it. When Polly was seated, he leaned over her shoulder while she thumbed through the pages one by one.

"This was a sizeable deposit made from the sale of land to the Duke of Willowbrook to later be sold as potential parcels of land for the growth of the community of Willowbrook," he said.

"Father always said he was sure Willowbrook would grow exponentially, until one day it would become a thriving city."

"And if things progress as they have been, your father's predictions will soon come true."

"Yes," Polly said, turning the page. "What is this?" she asked when she reached an empty page with a note scribbled at the top—*See addendum*. "What does this mean, Ethan?"

"I don't know. Turn to the back of the book. See if there's anything there."

Polly flipped through every page until, at the very back of the book, there was a page stuck to the back cover with Lord Springdale's private seal. It hadn't been broken, so no one had seen what was hidden there.

"Should we break the seal?" she asked, lifting her head to look at Ethan.

"Yes. We need to see what's beneath this paper."

Polly took a letter opener and gently lifted the seal that held the folded paper in place. "I don't want to read it, Ethan. I'm afraid."

"We have to, Polly. We have to know what we're facing."

Polly unfolded the paper so they could read it. She released a muffled cry, and Ethan wrapped his arm around her shoulders.

He felt the warmth of her, possibly for the last time. She wasn't going to be able to stand the sight of him after he was responsible for her father's murder.

Chapter Nine

"I DON'T BELIEVE this," Polly said, staring at the numbers on the page. "It can't be, Ethan. Father would never steal the Crown's money. He would never do something so dishonest."

It had taken her a long time to come to terms with what her father had done. But the proof was right in front of her.

"This is the work of a genius," Ethan said when he finished reading the page. "Your father detailed how he removed the money from the Finance Committee bank account. He itemized each transaction and where he sent the money. The entire amount was divided into smaller amounts and deposited in several foreign banks all over Europe. It will take someone forever to figure out where the money is."

"Can't someone just go to the banks and withdraw it? And put it back where it belongs?"

Ethan shook his head. "By now, he's probably moved each deposit several times to different banks. We'll never find all of it."

"Oh, Ethan," she cried. "How could he have done something so evil? It's not like he needed the money, was it?"

"No. Your father didn't need the money. He has more wealth than the two of you can spend in two lifetimes."

"Then why did he do it?"

"My guess would be to prove that he could. Your father is a genius."

Ethan took their glasses and refilled them, then sat with her on the sofa and held her.

"Surely he knew he couldn't get away with stealing from the Crown. Surely he knew what would happen to him if his theft was discovered," she said.

"Just as I think he knew it would be."

"What are you going to do, Ethan?"

"I don't have a choice, Polly. But before I do anything, I'm going to confront your father and force him to explain why he stole the money. I need him to account for his actions, and you need him to, as well."

"I don't know if I want to hear his excuse for what he did. He'll expect me to condone it, and I won't be able to."

"I know."

She sat with Ethan for a long time while he held her. They talked about what they had discovered and how their lives had changed in the blink of an eye.

Finally, the sun started to rise.

"I have to leave," Ethan said. "When do you expect your father to come home?"

"Perhaps tomorrow. More than likely, the next day."

"You will let me know when he arrives, won't you?"

Polly considered her answer. She wanted to lie and tell him she'd let him know the second her father returned, but she wasn't sure she could. If Ethan was anything, he was loyal to his queen and his country. Polly was signing her father's death warrant if she told Ethan when he returned home.

"Polly. You don't have a choice. You could be arrested if you hinder the authorities from doing their job."

"But I'll be responsible for my father's death if I don't protect him."

"Oh, sweetheart. I know how impossible this is for you. I know you would like to do anything other than help in the capture of your father."

"You mean, other than cause the murder of my father."

"Let's talk to him first," Ethan said. "Perhaps at least we'll understand why he did what he did."

"I'll never understand," she said. "He raised me. He taught me to be a good and decent person. He instilled honesty and trustworthiness in me from the moment I knew what those words meant. And he never let me forget his lessons."

"I know how difficult this is for you. Just don't forget, I'm here for you. We'll get through this together."

Polly couldn't reply. There was nothing to say. He would kill her father if he was convinced he had stolen money from the queen, and she would never be able to forgive him.

"Lock the ledger in the safe before I leave, Polly."

She took the ledger, and when it was safely locked away, she put the books back in front of it so no one would know the safe was there.

"Send Iris for me when your father arrives home, Polly. I don't want you to be alone with him. He'll realize the minute he sees you that something is wrong."

"All right," she replied, then watched Ethan leave the room and walk across the terrace. She watched until he'd gone through the hedgerow and she could no longer see him.

A part of her wished her father would never return. A part of her wished her father would get on a ship and leave London. Perhaps the queen wouldn't send anyone after him and he could live out his life in obscurity.

But that would never happen. Her father never ran from anything. No matter what. He would stay and face the consequences bravely. That was the kind of man he was.

Exactly the same as Ethan.

⇥⟫⟪⇤

ETHAN WORKED AT his bookshop all the next day. He had to keep himself busy. If he didn't, he'd go crazy thinking about Polly's father and what was going to happen when he returned.

He didn't want Polly to have to confront her father alone. But the day had gone by, and he hadn't shown up.

When Ethan closed his shop, he went to see Polly. He entered the garden by the usual way, by slipping through the gate in the hedgerow, then walking up the three steps and across the terrace to the French doors that opened to her father's study.

When he entered the room, he saw her sitting in the shadows. She turned her head and looked at him. Her eyes were rimmed with red circles and her cheeks were dotted with large splotches that confirmed she'd been crying.

He went to the liquor table and poured her a glass of wine, and himself a glass of brandy.

"I've already had several glasses of wine," she informed him, slightly slurring her words.

"Then I won't let you have too much more. Just enough to make sure you sleep tonight."

"I don't think it will help. I don't think anything will help."

"We'll see," he said, then sat down beside her. "Have you had anything to eat today?"

"I had a piece of toasted bread earlier. I wasn't hungry, but Iris forced me to eat something."

"Good," he said, leaning back against the cushions. As soon as he was comfortable, he placed his arm around her shoulders and brought her close to him.

She nestled closer and took a sip of her wine before the first tear trickled down her cheek.

Ethan handed her his handkerchief.

"Thank you," she said. "You would think I'd cried all my tears and wouldn't have any more left."

"You'd think," he replied, "but it's amazing how many tears we can produce."

"Then you must consider me a watering pot," she said.

"I consider you a very caring person."

"Oh, Ethan. I'm not sure that I can survive knowing what

father might have done."

"You can. You will."

"You can't possibly understand."

"But I can. I do. My family went through the same horrible experience as you are going through now."

Polly sat up and looked him in the eye. "When? How?"

"It happened when my father was a boy. His grandfather held the same position that your father holds right now, except my great-grandfather didn't have the moral fortitude your father hopefully has."

"Your great-grandfather held the same position as my father?"

"Yes."

"That means that you were…"

"Nobility. Yes. If we had been able to keep our title, my father would now be the Earl of Spelling and I would be Viscount Canton."

"What about your great-grandfather? What did the Crown do to him?"

"He committed suicide before they could do anything to him. He left my great-grandmother and my grandfather to face our family and friends alone, and my grandfather to struggle with what his father had done. I don't think he ever got over it."

"Oh, Ethan," she said on a sigh.

"My father, however, is made of sterner stuff. He picked himself up and started his own business."

"He opened a bookshop," she said.

"Yes. The Essex Bookshop. He wanted to show the public that just because his grandfather had tarnished our name, he was still proud of it. It took him a while to make a go of it, but, thanks to my mother's dowry, they didn't starve."

"She sounds like an extraordinary woman."

"She was. She loved my father with every inch of her being. And she stood beside him through everything he went through."

"Maybe I can meet him one day."

"Maybe," Ethan said, then held her closer. "Would you like to go for a walk in the garden before you retire for the night?"

"I would love to," she said, and rose when he held out his hand, then walked with him out the French doors and across the terrace.

The night was beautiful, warm, and the brisk breeze from earlier in the day had died down.

When they reached the pond, they stopped and watched the swans float on the water. Their heads were down and they were retiring for the night. Everything was so peaceful that Ethan could do nothing but hope that life would not change, even though he knew it would. It was bound to. They had much turmoil to face yet.

He took Polly in his arms and turned her so she faced him, then lowered his head and kissed her.

She met his kiss with as much passion as he shared with her. She skimmed her hands up his chest and wrapped her arms around his neck. Everything he demanded of her, she returned to him twofold. She let his arms skim over her back and then down her arms. She clearly welcomed his touch and encouraged his contact. When he lifted his mouth from hers, she breathed a ragged gasp in an effort to fill her starving lungs with air.

"I shouldn't have let you do that," she said.

"I should have stopped earlier, but we are perfect together. You affect me unlike anyone I've ever met."

"No. I don't. I can't."

"But you do. I thought it was only me who was affected by your kisses. But you are just as affected."

"Don't say that, Ethan. It's not possible. We can't afford to care for each other. I can't risk caring for you."

"I know you're correct," he said. "But I'm afraid it's already too late."

"No, it can't be. How are we going to survive when we can no longer be together?" she asked.

He shook his head. "I don't know. I don't know if we'll be able to."

"I can never love you. How can I when I know you're going to kill my father?"

She was right. He wished she wasn't, but he already knew that if they discovered her father was guilty of stealing from the government, he had to kill him. That was what he had been hired to do, and if he didn't, someone else would, and he wouldn't be able to stop them. He wouldn't *want* to stop them. It was what her father deserved.

"I need to take you back inside," he said, then wrapped his arm around her and led her back to the library.

When they were inside, he turned her to face him. "The *minute* your father comes home, send Iris for me. I don't want you to face him on your own. I need to be with you."

"But maybe I can—"

"No, Polly. You can't. I know how your father is going to react. I don't want you to be alone with him."

"All right," she finally agreed, and Ethan left her.

Somehow, he knew that tomorrow was going to be their last day together. There would be no others.

She was right. She could never love the man who had killed her father.

CHAPTER TEN

Ethan spent most of the next day watching the door, waiting for Iris to come to the shop. He'd informed his helpers that he would be called away and they should take over, then lock up at closing time if he hadn't returned.

Bloody hell, he hoped and prayed he wouldn't have to kill Polly's father in front of her. For the first time, he didn't want to be the one who the queen relied on to play judge, jury, and executioner.

Lunchtime came and went, and there was still no sign of Iris.

"Aren't you going for lunch, Mr. Essex?" Mrs. Tenpin asked when she and Mr. Tumberly returned from eating.

"No, I'm not hungry today. I'll eat something later."

He'd barely finished his sentence when the bell above the door jingled, and Iris entered the bookshop. Her eyes were wide with fear, and she was as frightened as Ethan had ever seen her.

"I have to leave now," he told his employees, and headed for the door.

Iris followed him as he left.

"Is her father there?"

"Yes, Mr. Essex."

"Has your mistress told you what is going on?"

"Yes, Mr. Essex. But I can't believe it. Lord Springdale could never do what the mistress thinks he did."

"Let's hope not, Iris."

They reached the hedgerow, and Ethan entered like he always did. "Where are they? In the library or Lord Springdale's study?"

"In the study, Mr. Essex."

Ethan headed for the study and told Iris to go in through the library. He didn't want her nearby.

He slowly, silently opened the French doors and stepped into the room.

Lord Springdale saw him the moment he entered.

"What the hell is going on?" Polly's father said, then ran to his desk and opened the top drawer. "Who are you?"

"Don't!" Ethan yelled, and lifted his arm. He had his gun in his hand and aimed at Lord Springdale. "Leave your gun in the drawer and step around your desk. Polly, come over here."

Polly took several steps until she reached him.

"Polly?" her father asked, obviously confused by his daughter's betrayal. "What are you doing?"

"I'm sorry, Papa."

Ethan pushed Polly behind him so she wouldn't be exposed.

"Who are you?" the marquess asked.

"I'm Ethan Essex. I own The Page Turner Bookshop. I'm also a special agent for Her Majesty, the queen."

"You're what?"

"I am a special agent for the queen."

"What are you doing in my home?"

"I was sent to find proof that you had stolen money from the Finance Committee."

"That is preposterous. I haven't stolen money from the queen."

"Are you sure?"

Lord Springdale became angry. He fisted his hands until his knuckles turned white. "Of course I'm sure! I would never take money from the Finance Committee."

"We found proof that you did, Papa," Polly said, stepping out from behind Ethan. Tears ran down her cheeks and her words caught on a strangled breath.

"That's a lie! You couldn't have! Because I didn't take any money. I would never steal from the queen. You, more than anyone, should know that, Pauline."

"I thought so, Papa. Until I saw the proof."

"Where is this proof? I want to see it."

"Get the ledger, Polly," Ethan said.

She walked to the bookshelf and removed the books, then opened the safe and took out the ledger.

"Place it on the desk, Polly, and open it to the last page."

Lord Springdale rose. "Why do you want it open to the last page? There's nothing there."

"Yes, there is, Papa," Polly said, then opened the ledger.

Before Lord Springdale reached the desk, Ethan opened the drawer and removed the pistol that was hidden there. Polly's father sat in the chair and pulled the ledger closer to him. He studied the paper and his eyes opened wide in shock.

"Where did this come from?"

"We assume it came from you," Ethan replied. "It was sealed with your seal. Your daughter broke it open."

Lord Springdale lifted his gaze and locked it with his daughter's.

"It's true, Papa. The paper was sealed with your seal."

"It couldn't have been," he said, then folded the paper and put the wax seal back together. "Who the hell could have done this?"

"Are you saying that you didn't?"

"Of course I didn't! Just as I didn't write this letter! This isn't my handwriting!"

"It certainly looks like yours," Ethan argued.

"But it isn't. Look." The marquess pointed to several of the words. "See how the tail on my *Y* goes straight down? Whoever wrote this slanted his *Y* at an odd angle. And look at the way he made his 8. That's probably the most obvious difference."

Ethan leaned over and compared the different pages.

"I'll grant you," Lord Springdale said, sitting back in his chair, "whoever wrote this did a damn fine job of it, but not perfect."

Ethan compared the numbers. They were noticeably different. "Do you have any idea who might want to frame you for the theft of that much money?"

Lord Springdale shook his head. "I haven't the vaguest idea. It could be anyone on the committee."

"Why do you think it's someone on the committee?" Ethan asked.

"They're the only ones who have access to the records. Besides the queen."

"I think we can eliminate her from our list of suspects," Ethan said. "Is there anyone else you think we can eliminate?"

Polly's father scanned the paper again. "Allow me to study this for a moment. At first glance, it looks rather complicated. There are some members of the committee that aren't mentally capable of organizing such complicated plans, but I will have to look at this closer to make sure."

"Of course," Ethan said. "I will give you until tomorrow. I will bid you a good night and see you in the morning." He walked to the French doors that led to the terrace.

"Mr. Essex," Lord Springdale said, stopping him from leaving. "Does this mean you believe I am innocent of all charges?"

"This means I am giving you a reprieve until I find definite proof of your guilt."

"And if you find such proof? What did Her Majesty assign you to do?"

"Kill you."

Lord Springdale's face paled. "Which you could have done the moment I returned from London."

"No, my lord. Which I would have done before you returned from London."

"Why didn't you?"

"Thank your daughter for convincing me to give you a

chance to prove that you are innocent."

Lord Springdale looked at his daughter with as much love as Ethan had ever seen on a father's face.

Ethan turned to leave. "Until tomorrow," he said.

"I'll walk you out," Polly said with a choked voice.

He held out his hand, and Polly took it. Together, they walked out the French doors and to the opening in the hedgerow. When they were out of sight, Ethan turned her in his arms and kissed her.

The depth of his kiss startled him, as it no doubt did her. She wrapped her arms around his neck and clung to him as if she was in fear of falling. She held him as if she might lose him, but she needn't have a care in that regard. She would never lose him. He would never leave her. He couldn't. He loved her too much.

When he broke off their kiss, she asked, "Are you convinced of my father's innocence?"

"Let's just say there's more doubt in my mind than there was before."

"He didn't do it, Ethan. I know he didn't."

"For your sake, I hope he didn't. And more important than that, I hope he can figure out who did."

"Even if Father can convince Her Majesty that he didn't steal the money, do you think she will take his word that he's innocent, or do you think it's so important that someone pays for that large a sum to have been stolen that she will punish him as an example for anyone else who thinks to do the same thing in the future?"

Ethan shook his head. "The queen is a fair-minded person. I have faith that she won't have him killed, but that doesn't mean she won't strip him of his land and title, and take away every pound he has and leave him penniless."

"That will kill Father."

"That will be the intent."

"Oh, Ethan," she moaned, then wrapped her arms around his middle. "Will you come early tomorrow?"

"As early as I can. I have a shipment of books coming in, and I have to be at the shop to unload them. Then I'll come to see what your father has figured out before I leave for London. I'll need to speak to Her Majesty."

Polly stood on tiptoe and kissed Ethan a final time, then turned and went back to the house. He didn't know how this was going to end, but he knew he would always be here for her.

There was no other place he wanted to be.

ETHAN MADE HIS way to London the next day and rode to Buckingham Palace. He left his horse and went directly to Her Majesty's apartments.

"Essex." Rupert Blackheart greeted him when Ethan reached the queen's rooms.

"Please inform the queen that I am here to see her."

"Of course. Was your mission completed successfully?"

"I'd like to see Her Majesty. Now."

"Yes, sir," Blackheart said, then knocked on the queen's door and entered. He returned in a matter of seconds. "Her Majesty will see you now."

Ethan followed Blackheart and entered the queen's sitting room. "That will be all, Blackheart," she said, then waited until he closed the door after himself. "Pour us each a whisky, Essex."

Ethan poured the queen a glass of her preferred liquor and one for himself. He waited until she indicated that he should sit, then sat across from her. He waited for her to take a swallow before he spoke.

"Did you complete your task?"

"No, Your Majesty. I didn't."

"You weren't convinced of his guilt?" she asked.

"I was not."

She drank more of her whisky. "Go on."

"I discovered the ledger that had the amounts that Lord Springdale supposedly took, then deposited, but upon close inspection, I noticed several discrepancies."

"What discrepancies?"

"For one thing, the handwriting didn't match. Oh, it was quite similar, and if I hadn't been looking for differences, I doubt I would have realized there were several. And the amounts were all listed in detail, exactly as they'd been in the front of the book, but the person who had entered them omitted certain details, such as the bank where they were deposited, and where he intended to move them."

"Move them?"

"Yes, Your Majesty. It is my assumption that the amounts stolen from the Finance Committee have been moved to banks all over Europe."

"Oh my," she said. "Is there anything else?"

"Yes, Your Majesty. I confronted Lord Springdale with the proof I had that he stole from you, and the expression of horror and disbelief on his face was quite convincing. I think my accusations came as a total surprise to him."

"If they hadn't?"

"I would have found him guilty and followed your orders."

"I believe you." Her Majesty took another swallow of her whisky. "What are you going to do now?"

"I'm going to get a sample of each committee member's handwriting and compare it to Springdale's."

"Excellent idea."

"It may take me a few days. I have some business to take care of at Willowbrook before I can return."

"That's all right. I've dismissed the Finance Committee for now."

"Do they know what has happened?"

"They know something is wrong, but I don't think they know what it is."

Ethan prepared to leave. "Does Your Majesty have anything

else?"

"No, Essex. I'm grateful for your caution."

"Thank you, Your Majesty." Ethan stood, bowed, and went to the door. "I will return when I know more."

He left and went for his horse. Before he left London, he rode into the city to visit his father. It had been a long time since he'd seen any of his family. They chatted for nearly an hour. He had so much to tell his father. Ethan caught up on all the family affairs, as well as the latest books that had come out and what people were buying.

When he realized it was getting late, he left to return home. He'd wanted to get back before dark, but at this rate, the sun would be low in the sky before he reached Willowbrook.

Ethan pushed his horse to travel faster than he probably should have, considering how dark it was getting, but he was in a hurry to reach home and tell Lord Springdale and Polly what the queen had said. He wanted Springdale to know that she, too, had her doubts as to his guilt.

Suddenly, a loud pop sounded, and Ethan felt a burning sensation in his chest. Immediately there was another pop and he felt another burning sensation, this time in his shoulder.

He slumped over his horse and held on to the saddle with all the strength he had. A third pop sounded, this time causing his arm to burn, and he lost his grip and fell to the ground.

He lay still as heavy footsteps neared him, and waited until a man's booted feet stopped beside him.

There was nothing remarkable about the boots, except for a scuff mark on the right side of the right foot. It was as if the man spent most of his time working at a desk and had worn the polish off when he crossed his feet.

Ethan lay still when the man's foot moved back then swung forward. He was going to kick him. With three bullets in him, Ethan knew he dared not try any defensive maneuvers. If he made the slightest sound, the killer would know he was still alive, and he'd shoot him a final time.

He prepared himself for the pain he knew was coming and didn't make a sound when the assassin kicked him. Thankfully, the man assumed he was dead.

Ethan lay still as death as the man stood there for a moment, then turned and walked away.

He didn't move for several agonizing minutes until he heard the man mount his horse and ride away.

Ethan had lost a lot of blood, and called for his horse in a weak voice. The gelding was well-trained and followed the command. When he stopped at Ethan's side, Ethan struggled to his feet. With one arm, he swung himself over the saddle and managed to get atop the horse.

The horse followed his instructions and took him to Springdale Hall. As the horse moved, Ethan simply hung on with the little strength he had. He remembered nothing after about the first three steps forward. Then he slumped over the horse's neck and knew no more.

CHAPTER ELEVEN

"I THOUGHT MR. Essex would have returned by now," Polly's father remarked as they sat in the library after dinner.

Polly had tried to keep him occupied with talk of the recent growth of the town of Brookfield over the past few months, but his mind was focused on Ethan and what he'd discovered in London. Polly couldn't blame him, but she knew it was only making him more nervous.

Finally, they heard a commotion in the foyer, and her father focused on the door, waiting for Sedgewick, their butler, to introduce Ethan. Within moments there seemed to be more commotion than usual, and instead of Sedgewick, a footman knocked, then opened the door.

"My lord."

"Yes?" her father answered.

"You need to come at once. The stable hands found a wounded rider. He's hurt bad, and Sedgewick sent for the doctor."

"Who is it, do you know?"

"No, my lord, but Sedgewick recognized him. He sent the men carrying him to one of the guest rooms. He's been shot more than once."

Polly didn't wait for her father to move. She knew without being told that it was Ethan.

She raced across the foyer, then up the stairs. The men carrying the wounded man were placing him on the bed.

"Ethan," she cried, then ran to the bed.

"He's badly hurt, my lady," a stable hand said.

"What happened to him?"

"Someone shot him."

Polly released a muffled cry, then reached for Ethan's hand and held it. "Send for water and cloths and bandages and anything else the doctor will need. Remove his boots, jacket, waistcoat, and shirt."

The servants scattered to follow her orders, and when a basin of water arrived, she wet a cloth and wiped his face.

He didn't move. At first Polly wasn't sure he was even breathing, but when the men lifted him to remove his clothes, he moaned. It was a pitiful sound.

"Is he alive?" her father asked, coming into the room.

"Yes, Papa. But barely," she answered through the tears that were streaming from her eyes. "He's been shot three times. Who would do something like this?"

"Whoever stole the money," her father said. "They must have been alerted as to what we'd discovered and were desperate to silence him."

When the men had removed Ethan's shirt, Polly wiped his chest. She wanted to remove as much of the blood as she could.

"You shouldn't be tending him, Pauline. We have servants to do that."

"No, I will do it."

Before her father could say anything more, the door opened and the doctor entered.

"Dr. Edwards," Polly greeted him. "I'm so glad you're here."

The doctor hurried to Ethan and inspected his wounds. "I will need some boiling water, alcohol, and a bottle of whisky."

Polly nodded to Sedgewick, and he gave the order to the servants.

"Now, my lady, I insist that you leave the room so I can

work. If I'm correct, there are two bullets that need to come out. The third went cleanly through. But I need to work fast. If the young man is fortunate, I can get the bullets out before he wakes. Either way, it's imperative that I stop the bleeding before he bleeds out. Now go."

Polly didn't want to leave Ethan, but her father took her arm and led her from the room. "Is there anyone here who can assist me?" she heard the doctor ask, and Sedgewick answered.

She didn't hear any more because the door closed behind her, and her father escorted her down the stairs. He led her to the closest room so they could hear the doctor when he was finished and came down. But for the next hour or more, it wasn't the doctor's footsteps they heard, but servants running up and down the stairs to fetch more water, or bandages, or anything else the doctor needed.

Thankfully, Sedgewick sent one of the servants down at regular intervals to inform them of Ethan's condition. What Polly was most interested in hearing was that Ethan was still alive.

FINALLY, THE DOCTOR came down. He explained that he'd done everything he could. He also gave them instructions on Ethan's care. He was to remain in bed for a minimum of three weeks. They were to change his dressings at least once a day, he was to have no solid food for the first week, only liquids and soft foods, and finally, they should watch for fever. Dr. Edwards would return to check on him.

Polly only listened with one ear. She was too anxious to escape to be with Ethan. The minute she could, she raced across the foyer and up the stairs, ran down the hallway to the room where he lay, and opened the door.

She stopped short when she saw him on the bed. He was more pale than before, and seemed more fragile than she thought he could possibly be. Huge tears filled her eyes and spilled over her lashes.

"Oh, sweetheart," she said, rushing to the bed and kneeling at his side. She reached for his hand and held it, remembering the precious times he'd held her hand to comfort her. She couldn't tell if he was breathing or not and was worried that he would stop and she would lose him. That thought scared her to death.

She said a prayer that God would let him live, then rose and rinsed a cloth in the fresh water one of the maids had just brought in. She placed it on his forehead and wiped the perspiration from his face.

He didn't move. It was as if he didn't know that she was there.

The door opened, and her father entered. "How is he?"

"Oh, Papa," she said. "He can't die. I can't let him die."

"I know you're fond of him, Pauline, but you have to prepare yourself for what will likely happen. Dr. Edwards all but said he probably won't survive. He's been injured too severely."

"No," she said. "He'll live. I won't let him die."

Polly became more agitated. The thought of Ethan dying was more than she could bear to consider.

"You are not forming an attachment to this man, are you, Pauline?"

"I've more than formed an attachment, Father. I love him."

"No! I refuse to allow you to think you might love him. He's a commoner. He's not of our standing. He's nothing! He's a nobody! A shopkeeper!"

"He's an agent of the queen. He's one of her most trusted men."

"He's a hired assassin. Assigned to assassinate *me!*"

"He's done everything he could to save you! Including possibly giving up his life to prove that you're innocent."

The door opened and Sedgewick entered. "Do you require anything, my lord?"

"No, Sedgewick," the marquess said. "I was just leaving."

Sedgewick stood back so her father could leave. When he was gone, the butler closed the door again. "Do you require anything, my lady?"

"I would like some tea, Sedgewick. If Father mentions he intends to visit Mr. Essex again, please advise him that he is not welcome, that his outbursts upset our patient."

"Yes, my lady. I'm sure his lordship won't bother you again."

"Thank you, Sedgewick."

"Yes, my lady. I'll send Iris in with your tea."

"Thank you," Polly said, then sat in the chair beside Ethan's bed and held his hand.

Sedgewick closed the door behind him, and Polly dropped her head to her hands and let the tears flow. She'd known her father's reaction would be what it was. She knew that he wouldn't consider Ethan good enough for her. Her father wouldn't think love played any part in marriage. Only title and rank and wealth.

"Don't worry, Ethan. I won't let him stop us from loving each other. I won't."

Polly placed another cool cloth on Ethan's forehead and placed her fingers on his cheek.

"Are you all right, my lady?" Iris said when she entered the room. "The staff heard your father shouting all the way to the kitchen."

"I'm sure they did," Polly said, then took the cup of tea Iris handed her.

"Now everyone knows your feelings for Mr. Essex. And they are pleased for you. He's so well-liked in the village."

Polly tried to stop more tears from falling but failed miserably.

"Cook sent up some bread and meat. She said you ate hardly anything for dinner."

"I'm not hungry, Iris."

"You need to eat, my lady. This is bound to be a very long night."

Polly placed her hand on Ethan's forehead. It was warmer than it had been earlier, but not so warm it seemed dangerous.

She placed another cool cloth on his forehead, then sent Iris for more cold water. She didn't know what she'd do if he ran a fever. Dr. Edwards was fearful of that happening.

POLLY TENDED HIM all through the night. Dr. Edwards returned later, as he'd promised, and gave her more instructions. She was to constantly rinse the cloths she put on Ethan's forehead with cold water if she had some. He sent a footman below stairs for a bottle of whisky and a bottle of wine. He poured some wine in a glass and showed her how much laudanum to add to the wine. This was to keep Ethan sedated so he didn't wake up and tear open his stitches.

She was also to talk to him so he had something to concentrate on. Many people didn't think a patient who was unconscious was able to hear, but Dr. Edwards said that wasn't the case. They couldn't respond, and it was debatable whether they could remember what had been said to them, but he was of the opinion that an unconscious patient knew when someone spoke to them. It made them realize that they weren't alone.

The doctor left but promised to return in the morning. When he was gone, Iris went down for a tea tray and a bite for Polly to eat. Polly dismissed the footman standing guard and was left alone with Ethan. She sat in the chair beside his bed, then reached out and held his hand.

"Ethan," she said, leaning over the bed. "I don't have much time before Iris returns, but I want to tell you how desperate I am that you survive." Her eyes filled with tears and no matter how hard she tried to keep them from spilling over her lashes, they ran in little rivers down her cheeks. "You know I can't live without you. I'd be lost without you. I love you too much to try to spend even one day without you."

She rinsed another cloth in cold water and placed it on his forehead. "Did you see who shot you? If you did, we'll find him and make him pay for trying to kill you. He's probably the same person who framed Father."

Polly took another cloth and soaked part of it in clean, cold water and placed it on Ethan's blue lips. Dr. Edwards had said that was one way to get a little liquid down him, and he needed to drink something. Anything.

"Father was here earlier. Did you hear us? We argued. He's as stubborn as ever. But I think I got the better of him. I stood up to him and wouldn't let him beat me down. You would have been proud of me."

Suddenly, Ethan struggled the slightest bit, and Polly placed her hand on his uninjured shoulder. She had to keep him still. She couldn't let him tear his wounds open.

He moaned and moved as if he was agitated. "Lie still, Ethan."

She placed her hand on his forehead and pulled it away. He was burning hot. How had it happened so quickly? She placed another cloth on his forehead and on his neck as Iris entered the room with a tea tray.

"Bring up more cold water, Iris, and get all the ice Cook has available. Then send a footman to help us."

"Yes, my lady."

Iris set the tea tray down and left the room. A minute later, a footman entered the room.

"Hold him down," Polly instructed the footman. "Lie still, Ethan. Just relax. Don't move."

Iris returned with a bucket of ice, and Polly put chunks of it in several towels and tied the ends together. She surrounded Ethan in ice and placed one towel on each of his wrists, his neck, and his forehead.

For hours the staff ran for more ice. Polly surrounded him with it. Ethan continued to struggle to free himself. He thrashed and twisted about while his fever raged.

The sun set, then rose again the next morning, and Ethan continued to thrash on the bed. Finally, after what seemed an eternity, he collapsed on the bed and lay still—so still that at first Polly feared he was dead. She leaned over him and placed her hand to his mouth, then exhaled a huge sigh of relief when she realized he was breathing. She felt his forehead and couldn't stop a small cry from escaping. His fever had broken.

"Oh, Ethan," she cried. Tears filled her eyes and trickled down her cheeks. "His fever broke," she told Iris. "His fever broke."

"We should remove the ice, then, and cover him up."

They called for more footmen and took Ethan to the next room, away from the mattress that was wet with melted ice and wouldn't dry anytime soon. When they had everything moved, the footmen left and Polly and Iris were alone with Ethan.

"That was frightening," Iris said while Polly reached for Ethan's hand and twined her fingers with his.

"Yes," she said while she watched him sleep. At regular intervals, she checked to make sure he was still breathing, and sighed in relief when she realized he was.

"Why don't you lie down for a while and sleep, my lady? I'll keep watch and call you if he wakes."

"No, Iris. I'll sleep here. I'm going to have a cup of tea first, then I'll close my eyes and try to sleep."

"Very well, my lady. Do you need anything else?"

"No. You sleep for a bit first. Tomorrow will be another long day."

"Do you think he'll wake?" Iris asked.

"I hope not. The longer he stays asleep, the longer he won't be in pain."

Iris poured Polly a cup of tea and gave it to her, then said goodnight and left.

"You frightened me half to death, Ethan," Polly said. "I would like your word that you will never do that again. I can't survive such frights." She reached for his hand and held it. She knew it was impossible, but she imagined that he had squeezed her fingers.

She held his hand for several minutes longer and finished her tea. Then she leaned her head back against the cushion and slept still holding his hand.

CHAPTER TWELVE

"How is he?" Dr. Edwards asked when he entered the room the following morning.

"He had a fever last night," Polly answered. "We covered him in ice until it broke. I gave him small pieces of ice to suck on, and that seemed to help."

"Very good. That was just what he needed."

The doctor checked on Ethan, then changed his bandages. When he finished, he tried to get him to drink a little something. When that failed, he placed a small piece of ice in Ethan's mouth, the same as Polly had done the night before.

"Don't be surprised if his fever returns. That's normal. If it stays high for too long, you'll have to do the same that you did last night. Hopefully, though, it will come down on its own and you won't have to bother with so much ice."

Polly thanked the doctor for coming, then watched as he left the room.

"Did you hear the doctor, Ethan? He said you're doing well. I think he was surprised at how well. He doesn't realize how remarkable you are. He doesn't realize that you are one of the strongest people God ever made." She placed a fresh cloth on his forehead. "This should make you feel better."

While they were alone, she leaned over and kissed him. She knew she had to be careful that her father didn't walk in and catch her doing such a thing, but she doubted he would.

"Oh, Ethan. I just had a wonderful thought. Would you like it if I contacted your father and asked him to come see you? I know he'd like to come, if not to see you, to see your bookshop." She smiled. "That was a joke," she said. "Of course he'd like to come see you. That would be first on his mind, but I'm sure he'd like to see your bookshop, too."

Polly changed the cloth on his forehead, then sat in the chair beside him and held his hand. "Have I ever told you how handsome you are? Well, I think you are remarkably handsome, but if you ever say I said such a thing, I will deny it with every breath in my body. You'll think I fell in love with you because of your amazing good looks."

Polly carried on a one-sided conversation so long that her throat choked with emotion. Suddenly, she couldn't hold back the tears that consumed her. She felt them grow heavy in her breast, then build in her throat until they filled her eyes and spilled over her lashes, and violent sobs wracked her body. She'd tried to be strong for so long that she wasn't sure she could be strong any longer. She'd tried to be positive when deep inside she was so terrified that she couldn't breathe at times. She wasn't sure how much longer she could keep this façade in place before she shattered under the weight of it.

When every sob she'd bottled up was spent and gone, she lifted her head and wiped her face dry. It was then that she noticed it—Ethan's grip had tightened around her fingers.

She brought his hand to her lips and kissed his fingers. "Ethan?" she said, pleading with him to react, but he didn't. He lay quiet and unmoving. His hand was lax in hers, as if it had never changed. But she knew it had. She had to believe it had. Believing was the only thing that would keep her sane.

It was all she had to cling to.

ONE DAY TURNED to another, and still Ethan did not wake. The doctor told her this wasn't uncommon, that there were patients who stayed in an unconscious state because when they woke, the pain would be so severe they didn't want to face it. She looked at the wounds covering Ethan's body and was certain that was the reason for his sleeping.

On the third day, there was a knock on the door and Iris entered with a tall, distinguished-looking gentleman on her heels. Polly knew at a glance that this was Ethan's father.

"Oh, Mr. Essex," she said, rising to her feet. "I'm so glad you have arrived."

"Is he still alive?" he asked in a voice that sounded similar to Ethan's.

"Yes. Although he hasn't awakened yet."

"You must be Lady Pauline, the person who wrote me."

"Oh, yes. Forgive me. I should have introduced myself."

Ethan's father stepped closer to the bed and placed his hand on his son's forehead. "You've taken excellent care of my son. He doesn't seem to have a fever."

"No, sir. He ran a fever four days ago, then the next day, but we got it to come down with a great deal of ice, and he hasn't run a fever for two days now."

"Thank you. I don't want to think how I'd feel if I lost him."

A footman brought a chair over so Ethan's father could sit by his son.

"Do you know who tried to kill him?"

"Not yet. We're hoping that Ethan can tell us what he knows when he wakes."

"Was he on an assignment from the queen?"

Polly wasn't sure how to answer. She hadn't been certain his father knew what his son did for the queen, but obviously he was much more informed than she expected. Finally, she decided the truth was the best course to take.

"Yes, sir. He was."

Mr. Essex nodded, while Polly stood to change the cloths on

Ethan's forehead. When she sat back down, Ethan's father seemed to be studying her.

"You care for him, don't you?"

Polly lowered her gaze then nodded.

"My son is a lucky man, then," he said.

"Thank you, sir. I consider myself the one who is lucky."

Mr. Essex reached out and clasped Ethan's hand in his. "What do you think of my son owning a bookshop?"

"I think it's wonderful. He has a good head on his shoulders and will make a fine success of anything he puts his mind to."

"I see you're a loyal supporter of his. Has he shown you any of his children's books?" Polly's face must have betrayed her surprise, because he laughed. "He thinks I don't know about his writing ventures, doesn't he?"

"That's true. I see he wildly underestimates you."

"I've known for a very long time that my son was an exceptional young man. He never failed to impress me in any of his endeavors."

"From his description of you, you never failed to impress him either."

"Thank you, my lady. I appreciate hearing that."

They spoke for several more minutes, then Polly realized how remiss she had been. "Oh, Mr. Essex. I'm sure you're famished after your journey. Would you like to have me send up a tray, or would you like to go down and eat at the table?"

"If you don't mind, I would like to eat here with my son. I didn't come all this way only to be separated from him so soon."

Polly smiled. "Iris, would you bring more ice water up, and I'll talk to Cook to prepare a tray for Mr. Essex. We'll give you a few moments alone with your son."

"Thank you," he said. "I'd appreciate that."

Polly and Iris left the room and set about their tasks. Polly couldn't get over how similar Ethan was to his father, both in looks and mannerisms. Even their smiles and personalities were similar.

Polly could tell what Ethan would look and act like when he was older, and she was elated with the husband she would have.

❯❯❯❯❮❮❮❮

POLLY WOKE THE next morning when a stranger entered Ethan's room. She was an elderly lady and wore a uniform of sorts.

"Pauline," her father said from the open doorway. "This is Mrs. Cafferty. She will take over caring for Mr. Essex. You have done more than is required of you. It's not seemly for you to spend so much time alone with an unmarried man."

"I can't see where that is a problem, Papa. Mr. Essex is still unconscious. He can hardly be considered a threat to my virtue."

"That doesn't matter. It's simply not appropriate."

"I'm not leaving, Father. I am where I belong. If Mrs. Cafferty would like to stay to assist me, I welcome her company. But I am not leaving."

Just then, Ethan's father entered the room. "Is something wrong?" he asked.

"No, no. Nothing is wrong. Father just introduced me to the nurse he hired to assist in taking care of Ethan. Mr. Essex, this is Mrs. Cafferty. Mrs. Cafferty, allow me to present your patient's father, Mr. Essex."

"It's a pleasure to meet you."

After she introduced everyone, she looked down. Ethan's hand moved and his head turned from side to side.

"Ethan!" Polly rushed to Ethan's side and knelt beside him. "Ethan, can you hear me? Are you ready to wake up now?"

He moved on the bed and moaned. Before Polly could get the wine with laudanum Dr. Edwards had left for him, the doctor walked through the door.

"Is he waking?" he asked, coming over to check on his patient.

"Yes," Polly answered with tears forming in her eyes. "He's

94

waking."

She moved to the side of the bed and removed the cloth from Ethan's forehead. Then she stroked his hand and twined her fingers with his.

Dr. Edwards checked his breathing and the bandages. He removed them and replaced them with clean ones. Then he reached for a glass of water. "Here," he said, holding the glass to Ethan's lips. "Drink." Ethan opened his mouth and drank until Dr. Edwards removed the glass. "Not too much, Ethan."

Polly still held Ethan's hand and watched while he struggled to open his eyes. It took him several minutes to adjust to the light in the room, then his eyes moved from person to person.

"Papa?" he said in a hoarse voice that hadn't been used in nearly a week.

"Yes, Ethan," his father said. "Lady Pauline wrote me that you'd been injured, and I decided I'd better come to see you and make sure you got better."

"I'll be better soon."

"You need to rest for a while longer," Dr. Edwards said. "I've given everyone here strict instructions not to allow you to get out of bed one day shy of three weeks."

"Right now that sounds…doable," he said. "But I'm sure…I'll want to negotiate the…end time when I'm…feeling better."

"We'll discuss that later," the doctor said.

Ethan turned his gaze back to his father. "Have you been to my… bookshop yet?"

"No," his father answered. "I was going to go this afternoon. I can't wait to see what you've got."

"I think you'll…like it," Ethan said, then winced.

"Very well," the doctor said. "He's been awake long enough. Here." He held the glass of wine and laudanum to Ethan's mouth. "Drink this." Ethan drank a healthy amount before the doctor put the glass on the bedside table. "Do you remember how I showed you to mix the wine and laudanum, my lady?"

"Yes," Polly answered.

"Keep some ready to give him when he needs it."

She nodded her understanding.

"Now, it's time for my patient to get some rest. You can come back to see him after lunch, but not a whole crowd of you. Just two at a time."

"Iris, please show Dr. Edwards to the kitchen and have Cook give him something to eat. And Sedgewick," she instructed the butler, "show Mr. Essex the way to The Page Turner Bookshop."

"Yes, my lady," they all answered, then Sedgewick opened the door and they left.

"Come, Pauline," her father ordered. "You should leave now, too. Mrs. Cafferty will stay with Mr. Essex."

"That's all right, Papa. Mrs. Cafferty can go down now. I'll stay with Mr. Essex for a while first."

"*Pauline*," her father repeated in a much firmer voice. "Mrs. Cafferty will—"

"You can go now, Father. I will stay."

Polly knew her father would not argue with her in front of strangers, but he wasn't finished with her yet. She would hear about her disobeying him when they were alone.

"You can leave, Polly," Ethan whispered. "I'll be fine."

"I'm not going to leave you," she whispered back. "I'll never leave you." She reached for his hand and held it.

When she said no more to her father, he turned and left the room along with Mrs. Cafferty. Finally, Polly and Ethan were alone.

"Do you need more laudanum?" she asked.

"No. I want to stay awake for a while."

"I have missed you," she said, and meant every word. "You frightened me to death."

"I frightened myself, too. I wasn't sure I'd survive this. It was the closest I've ever come to dying."

"But you didn't, and I couldn't be more thankful," Polly said, leaning closer to him and kissing him.

"What were you and your father arguing about before I

woke?" he asked. "It sounded serious."

"It was nothing."

"I hate it when you refer to me as nothing," he said.

Polly couldn't help herself from laughing, which made him laugh at her.

"Ohh," he moaned, holding his side.

"Oh, I'm sorry," she said. "But that was your fault. You made me laugh."

"I'll know not to do that again for several weeks."

"That will teach you," she teased, then sobered. "What should we do?" she asked. "Do you know who shot you?"

Ethan shook his head. "I didn't have a chance to…see his face. Only his shoes. The right shoe was worn on the outside in two areas, as if he spent a great deal of time at a desk."

"That could be anyone," Polly said.

They sat together for a while longer until she could see Ethan was tiring. "You need to sleep now."

"Yes. Would you do me a favor?" he asked.

"Of course."

"Hand me the glass with laudanum, then send Mrs. Cafferty up. Let me sleep for a few hours, then bring your father up to see me. I'd like him to go to London for me."

"Of course." Polly lifted the glass of wine laced with laudanum to his lips and let him drink. It only took a few minutes before Ethan's eyes closed and he was asleep. Then Polly went down to send Mrs. Cafferty up and to find her father.

She didn't want to face her father again after their confrontation earlier, but she had no choice. They had to discover who had tried to kill Ethan before they tried again. And this time they might be successful.

CHAPTER THIRTEEN

POLLY SENT MRS. Cafferty up to sit with Ethan, then went in search of her father. She found him in his study.

"Do you have a moment, Papa?" she asked upon entering.

"Of course, Pauline," he said, then placed his pen on his ledger and closed the book. "What did you want?"

"I was discussing what Ethan thinks we should do about whoever it was who tried to kill him."

"Please, Pauline. The man's name is Mr. Essex. I would appreciate it if you referred to him as such."

"Ethan and I passed the 'mister' and 'my lady' point long ago, Father."

"I don't believe this," he said, becoming angrier by the second.

"Father, please. Can we forget this for a moment and talk about what we are going to do to prove your innocence?"

"Do you have an idea?"

"No, but Ethan does."

"What does he suggest?"

"He would like to speak to you in a little while. He needs to rest now, but after he wakes, he'd like to talk to you about going to London."

"To see the queen?"

"I believe so. He'll explain everything to you when he

wakes."

"Very well," her father said, then Polly turned to leave. "Pauline?"

She stopped. "Yes, Father?"

"Please, consider what you are doing. You are the daughter of nobility. You are the daughter of a marquess. I can't even consider the life you might lead if you stoop so low and consider marriage to a commoner."

"A happy one, Father. A very happy one."

With tears in her eyes, she left the room. As she rounded the corner, she met up with Ethan's father and Sedgewick in the front hall.

"Mr. Essex," she greeted him. "What did you think of Ethan's bookshop?"

"I was more impressed that I thought I would be. I knew his shop would be exemplary. He was raised working in a bookshop, so he knows the running of the business, but I had no idea it would be so impressive."

"It is, isn't it?"

"Yes. And he found two remarkable people to work in his shop. They asked after Ethan, and I told them what I could. I also told them that I would come to the shop tomorrow and make out an order. That was one job neither of them had done yet."

"Oh, thank you. I know Ethan will be relieved to hear that. Come, Mr. Essex. Would you like to join me for a cup of tea?"

"I would like that very much," he said, then followed her to a sitting room.

Polly ordered a tea tray, then poured when the tray came.

"I couldn't help but overhear your father's objections concerning my son," Mr. Essex said. "I'm sorry about that. I know how important titles are to the ruling class."

"Yes, Ethan explained that you were once a member of that class."

Mr. Essex smiled. "It was more difficult for my father. He was privileged for a large part of his life before those advantages were taken from him. I barely knew any of them. Ethan has only known the life of a commoner. He fits in a commoner's skin quite well."

"Yes, he does."

"I wanted to thank you for writing to me. I appreciate your thoughtfulness. I'm thankful things turned out as they have, and I'm glad I had this opportunity to see him. Who knows how long it would have taken me to get here otherwise?"

"I'm glad I got to meet you, too."

"I feel the same, my lady. It's obvious that you care for my son. Has he returned your feelings?"

"Yes," Polly answered. "We feel the same about each other."

"I'm glad," he said, "but I can't help but agree with much of what your father says."

Polly felt a knot form in her stomach. "Are you saying that you disapprove of our relationship?"

Mr. Essex shook his head. "I don't disapprove of the feelings you and Ethan have developed for each other. I would, however, like to caution you to consider everything you will be forced to give up."

"I am well aware of what I will be giving up, Mr. Essex, and I can assure you that there is not one thing I will miss. Not one."

Ethan's father smiled. "I think I believe you, my lady."

Polly reached for her future father-in-law's hand and squeezed it. "Thank you," she said.

They talked for several minutes longer until the door opened and Sedgewick entered. He informed Polly that Ethan was awake and would like to see her and Lord Springdale.

"Would you like to join us?" she asked Mr. Essex.

"I'd love to, but only as an observer. I just want to know what's going on without Ethan having to explain it again."

"Come with me, then," she said, then led the way from the room. They stopped to get her father first, then walked up the stairs and to Ethan's room.

"Father," Ethan said.

"I just came to hear what you had planned, not to interject," Mr. Essex said. "Pretend I'm not here."

Ethan smiled and rested his head on the pillow. Polly smiled back.

When the door was closed, Ethan focused on her father.

"Are you sure you're rested enough, Ethan?" she asked him.

"Yes. I need to tell your father what I found out."

Polly wanted to hold Ethan's hand, just to let him know she was there for him, but she couldn't with her father sitting next to her.

"Do you know who shot you, Essex?" the marquess asked.

"No. I didn't see his face," Ethan replied. "I only saw his feet. To be more precise, I only saw his shoes."

"His shoes?"

"Yes. After he shot me, I fell from my horse. I lay as still as I could when he came up to me. I held my breath and didn't move. That's when I saw his shoes. He pulled his right foot back and kicked me. I think he wanted to make sure I was dead, so I pretended that I was."

"Was there anything special about his shoes that you remember?"

"Yes. The heel and toe areas on the outside of his right shoe were worn, as if my attacker crossed his ankles as he worked at a desk."

"Are you saying that it may not have been one of the Finance Committee members?" the marquess asked.

"I don't know any member of the committee who would dare appear in public with their shoes in such a ratty condition. But to make sure, I'd like for you to eliminate the committee members first, then move on to the queen's staff."

"Wise plan. Her Majesty has several staff employed in her office."

"Yes. After you have eliminated the committee members, we can move on to those."

"How do you suggest we eliminate the committee members?"

"I think the fastest method would be to call a committee meeting," Ethan said. "Keep your eye out for anyone who is shocked to see that you're still alive, or that you haven't been arrested. Then, when they leave, examine every one of their feet. Their right foot in particular. If one of them has a scuffed right heel, don't do anything. Just make a note of that fact."

"Why do nothing? There wouldn't be a better time to arrest him."

"Perhaps not," Ethan said, "but we have to find out where he has the money hidden. As long as he thinks he's getting away with stealing such a sum, he'll either continue adding to it, or he'll gather it all together to take it with him wherever he intends to go."

"How do you know he intends to go somewhere?"

"Wouldn't you? Would you risk staying in England when it's only a matter of time until the queen figures out you stole such a large amount of money and are living a life well beyond your means?"

"No," the marquess answered. "Now, what do you want me to tell the queen?"

"Tell her that I was injured but I will be back in two weeks."

"You won't return for three weeks," Polly interrupted. "And not one day sooner."

"I don't think that's possible," Ethan said. "We can't let our thief remain free for that long without someone watching him. That someone has to be me."

"It can also be me," her father said.

"No disrespect intended, my lord, but are you sure you're able to keep an eye on our subject and follow him around the streets of London for three weeks?"

"Perhaps I can't follow him, but Scotland Yard has several well-trained officers who can keep an eye on him and report his every move."

"Yes," Ethan said. "That will work. So, your job will be to

discover the identity of our thief and keep an eye on him. Ask the queen for any assistance you need."

"I will," the Marquess of Springdale replied, then rose from his chair. "When do you suggest I leave?"

"Can you leave in the morning?"

Lord Springdale nodded.

"Thank you, my lord," Ethan said.

"Thank *you*, Mr. Essex. For allowing me the chance to prove my innocence. For not assuming that I was guilty and killing me."

"You have your daughter to thank for that, my lord. She's the one who was convinced that you were incapable of stealing anything. Especially one hundred thousand pounds."

The marquess looked at Polly and reached for her hands. He brought them to his lips and kissed them. "I am very proud of you, daughter."

"And I'm proud of you, Father," she replied.

"I will leave first thing in the morning," Lord Springdale said. "It will take me a day or more to get the committee together and check their shoes. Then another day to check the shoes of Her Majesty's staff. I'll let you know if I find our thief."

"Thank you," Ethan said as the marquess left the room. The minute Ethan's father was the only one in the room besides Polly and Ethan, Polly brought the glass of wine and laudanum to Ethan and lifted his head to help him drink.

"How did you know?" he asked taking several swallows.

"Oh, I don't know," she teased. "Perhaps it was the furrows on your forehead that got deeper and deeper the longer you talked. Or perhaps it was how your face lost its color as you spoke. Or perhaps it was—"

"See, Father?" Ethan said. "I should have chosen someone who wasn't as observant as Polly. Then I'd get by with more."

"You just remember that, sir," she said as Ethan's father laughed.

"Did you visit my bookshop today, Father?"

"I did," Mr. Essex replied.

"What did you think of it?"

"It's wonderful, son. I even took away a couple of ideas to implement in my store."

"Really?"

"Yes. Especially the wide array of stationery items you carry. While I was there, two customers came in to peruse your selection."

"Did they purchase anything?"

"Yes, they did. You have a lively business and two superb individuals working for you."

"Yes, I was very fortunate to have found them."

"Yes, you were," Polly said. "But now it's time for you to rest for a while. You can hardly keep your eyes open."

"I am a tad tired," Ethan said with his eyes already closed.

Polly straightened the covers over him, then she and Ethan's father left the room.

"I think he's probably already sleeping," Mr. Essex said.

"I think you're right," Polly replied. "You have a remarkable son, Mr. Essex. I don't know anyone who would be healing this quickly."

"He's always been tough like this. I just wish his mother was alive to see him all grown up."

"I'm sure you do," Polly said, knowing her father felt the same about her own mother.

CHAPTER FOURTEEN

Ethan struggled to open his eyes, and when he did, the sun shone so brightly that he was forced to close them. He waited a few seconds, then opened them again.

His first sight was of Polly sitting in her chair beside his bed. She had a pad of paper in her lap and was making some sketches. As if she realized he was watching her, she lowered her pencil and smiled at him.

"Good morning," she said.

"Good morning," he replied, then turned his gaze to the clock on the mantel. "Is that clock correct?"

"No, it speeds up each night at midnight and moves time along twice as fast until you wake up."

Ethan focused his gaze on Polly as she tried to keep from laughing. But he couldn't help it. He had to laugh, even though he knew his side would hurt when he did. "You have a wicked sense of humor, lady."

"And you, sir, are so easy to read you make it easy to tease you. I'd wager you've never slept so long in your entire life, have you?"

"No. Why on earth did you let me sleep so long?"

"Because you needed the rest," she replied. "Dr. Edwards left strict instructions."

"But he didn't mean I was supposed to sleep until noon."

"I think that's exactly what he meant. Now, let me ring for some tea and something for you to eat. Would you like to have breakfast or lunch?"

"What has Cook prepared me for breakfast?"

"I think she has broth of some kind and tea."

"What is for lunch?"

Without cracking a smile, she said, "I think she said she had a broth of some kind and tea."

Ethan rolled his eyes. "I would like coffee instead of tea, and breakfast instead of lunch. How does that sound?"

"It sounds perfect, although I'm not sure how you can prefer coffee over tea."

"The army did that to me. Ruined me for life."

Polly smiled, and it was the most beautiful sight Ethan had ever seen. He was reminded again of how much he loved her.

She rose and called for Iris, then instructed her to bring Ethan some coffee and breakfast. She sat back down when she returned.

"Has your father left for London yet?" Ethan asked.

"Yes. In fact, he should almost be there by now."

"And my father. Where is he?"

"He left to work at The Page Turner Bookshop. He said he was going to make out an order for you. Your workers told him that they had been quite busy the past few days."

"That is good."

"Yes."

Before he could ask any more questions, a maid entered with Ethan's coffee, and a pot of tea for Polly.

"Do you need some laudanum yet?" she asked.

"No, Polly. I'm afraid if I take some laudanum, I'll fall asleep again and miss out on dinner."

"Oh, I wouldn't let you miss out on dinner. Cook has some excellent beef broth cooking for you."

"And what else?"

"Oh, I think I heard her say something about some gruel. Or maybe that was what you would have for breakfast as a treat."

"You are in fine form this morning, aren't you?"

"Oh, I was in very fine form this morning, but you slept through my superb conversation. I was quite lively."

Ethan laid his head on the pillow and smiled. He wished he could move. He'd reach out and pull her in bed beside him and kiss her. Then he'd keep her in bed with him all day long.

Before he could ask her any more questions, a maid entered with his breakfast. Polly rose and helped arrange the food on a small table she moved by the bed.

She helped him sit up, and Iris placed a pillow behind him so Polly could feed him. He tried to eat by himself but couldn't manage. He was much weaker than he thought. Much more helpless.

"Don't move, Ethan," Polly said. "You'll start bleeding again, and we'll have to call for Dr. Edwards."

"Was he here this morning?"

"Yes. But you slept the entire time."

"I don't believe it."

"I wouldn't lie to you about that. Well, I would, but I'm not."

"Very funny," he said, then opened his mouth to accept her spoonful of broth. "You weren't kidding, were you?"

"About the broth?"

"Yes."

"No. But I see you'll get some custard for dessert. That should please you."

Ethan opened his mouth again and drank more broth.

When he was finished eating, Polly and Iris helped him lie down, and before he knew it, he was asleep again.

ETHAN COULDN'T BELIEVE it, but this was his normal routine for the first week. He didn't think it was possible for anyone to sleep so many hours during the day, but he did. It wasn't until the second week that he was able to stay awake for most of the morning. But he couldn't manage to stay awake during the afternoon. He slept several hours every afternoon, but Dr. Edwards had said that the rest plus a healthy liquid diet would help him heal faster.

The doctor came every day to change his bandages and make sure he didn't develop a fever. At the end of the second week, he gave Ethan permission to get out of bed and walk the halls. He even allowed him to climb down the stairs and sit on the terrace, but for no more than two hours a day.

He even allowed him to eat soft and semi-soft foods such as coddled eggs and cooked vegetables. The first time Ethan had a regular soft meal of mashed potatoes, vegetables, and cooked apples, he thought Polly hung the moon for making it happen. No dinner had never tasted so heavenly.

After he finished his meal, Polly took him out on the terrace and pulled her chair beside his. Ethan wrapped his uninjured arm around her shoulder. She leaned against him and placed her head in the crook beneath his chin.

"I've waited weeks to sit here like this with you," he said, leaning over to kiss her forehead.

"And I've been waiting for you to be able to sit here with me."

"Has my father returned from the bookshop yet?"

"No. He's been spending more and more time there. He mentioned that he expected a cartload of books to arrive today."

"Are you certain he said a cartload of books? Not just a box of books, but a cartload?"

Polly smiled at him. "No, maybe he said two cartloads," she teased him. "Yes, now that you mention it, I'm sure he said two cartloads."

"Very funny," he chided her, pulling her a little closer and holding her tighter.

She laughed, then lifted her head and kissed his cheek. "Yes, he said a cartload, but I'm sure he only meant a box."

"Then you don't know my father. If he said a cartload of books, that's what he meant—a cartload of books."

"Are you worried you won't have enough money to pay for them? Is that the problem?"

"No, money isn't the problem. I'm not a poor man, Polly. I'm worried about having to purchase another building, so I have enough room to display all the books he ordered. His love of books sometimes gets in the way of his common sense. He's like a lady who goes to the store to pick up a few colors of thread. She goes for three or four colors but comes home with three or four dozen skeins in several colors that she doesn't really need. He collects books like some people collect paintings."

Ethan heard voices from the foyer.

"Well, I think he's home," Polly said. "Now you can ask him yourself."

Ethan waited until his father came out onto the terrace. "Good evening, Papa."

"Good evening, Lady Pauline. Ethan," his father said. "You have no idea how good it is to see you upright, son."

"You have no idea how good it feels to be upright. Have you had your dinner?"

"Yes. Mr. Tumberly, Mrs. Tenpin, and I stopped at the café to eat after we closed the shop."

"Polly said you got in a load of books today."

"Yes. Not that many, though. Only three boxes. You had several empty spots on some shelves, and they needed to be filled. Is that a problem, Ethan?"

Ethan smiled. "No, not at all. Thank you for doing that for me. I can't wait until I'm well enough that I can come down to the shop. It's odd. I miss it."

"That's not odd. It's normal. That's your business. You created it. It's yours. By the way," his father said, "have you heard anything from Lord Springdale?"

"No. Not yet. But I expect to hear from him any day now."

"Do you think he's found the man who tried to kill you?"

Ethan shook his head. "If he had, I think he would have sent word immediately."

"How long have you been up?" his father asked.

"Oh, no," Ethan sighed. "Don't tell me you're keeping track of me too? Usually I just have to worry about Polly."

Polly and his father laughed. "It's just that you look a little pale," he said. "I just don't want you getting too tired."

"That's thoughtful of you, but it's just the moonlight," Ethan replied. "It makes everything look pale."

"If you say so," his father said. "Well, I'm going to go to bed. Tomorrow will be a long day. We'll have to unpack all those boxes of books."

"Good night," Polly and Ethan told his father, and he returned to the house.

"I do believe your father is correct, Ethan," Polly said. "You do look a little pale. I think you need to go back to bed."

Ethan laughed. "I was afraid he'd give you ideas," he said, struggling to his feet. "But first I'd like to walk in the garden for a bit. Would you mind?"

"No, but only as far as the first bench," she said with a smile and a nod.

Ethan matched her smile, and they began to move along the path. When they reached the first bench, Polly turned around. Ethan matched her steps, but instead of going back, he turned her to face him. He gathered her in his arms and lowered his head until his lips met hers.

He'd waited what seemed an eternity to be able to kiss her. She tasted like honey and a hint of the sweet tea she'd sipped earlier.

"I love you, Ethan," she said when he lifted his mouth from hers.

"And I love you," he replied, "but I'm not sure that's so wise, Polly."

She pulled back a few inches. Frown lines were etched deeply across her forehead. "What do you mean?"

"I've had a lot of time to think things over lately."

"And what have you been thinking about?"

"You and me," he said. "What your father said."

"You heard him?"

"Yes. I heard him, and he was right. We don't come from the same worlds, Polly. I'm a commoner. A bookshop owner. I'll never be anything more. I'll be a common laborer the rest of my life."

"And you'll write books. And I'll illustrate them. We'll fit together like hand and glove."

"But I can't give you anything more. You'll never be able to take your place in Society again. We won't be invited to any social events. The class of people that have always meant so much to your father will no longer include you in their circle of friends."

"Listen to yourself, Ethan. You're describing what my father wants for me. Not what I want for myself. All that is important to me is that you will always love me. Will you? Do you promise that you will always love me?"

"You know I will," he replied. "I love you today, but not as much as I will love you tomorrow or the day after that. Except I'm afraid that will not be enough for you. I am afraid that one day you'll wake up and want more, and I won't be able to give it to you."

"Then you can remind me of this conversation and the oath I gave you that you will always be enough for me. That your love will always be as much as I'll ever want or need. Do you hear me?" Polly said. "You can remind me of this conversation, and it will be all that I'll need to remember the vow I made to you. I love you and always will."

"Oh, my love," he said, and leaned down to kiss her. His kiss was filled with every bit of the passion he felt for her. He opened his mouth over hers and encouraged her to accept him for what he was, and what he offered her.

OVER THE NEXT two weeks, Ethan went to The Page Turner Bookshop for a few hours every day. Every time when he came home, he brought with him another book he'd written, and Polly spent her free time illustrating it. She couldn't get over how good his books were. She was certain children of every age would love each of them, and she hoped her drawings would keep the little ones interested in them.

Ethan assured her that they would. He said he was impressed by her drawings, and she tended to believe him. In her opinion, she'd never done better work.

At the end of the second week, she entered his room to find him up and dressed as if he were ready to travel.

"Where do you think you are going?"

"To London."

"London?"

"Yes," he answered, and handed her a message from her father.

"He thinks he found the man who shot you?" she asked when she'd read the missive.

"Yes, but he needs me to look at the shoes and see if I recognize them."

"And you were going to go alone?"

"I don't want you anywhere near this monster, Polly. He's dangerous. He has a lot to lose and won't hesitate to eliminate any of us who get in his way."

"How soon are you leaving?" she asked.

"I should be ready in half an hour."

"Very well. I'll have Sedgewick put plenty of pillows and blankets in the carriage to make your trip as comfortable as possible, and have Cook pack you a lunch so you can eat on the way."

"Thank you," he said, kissing her on the cheek.

"What? You expected me to send you to ride all the way to London without any comfort?"

"No. But I didn't expect you to make it so easy on me," he answered.

"I know you too well by now to not know how useless it is to argue with you."

He kissed her again, and Polly left to room to get ready. She didn't have much time.

Thirty minutes later, Ethan descended the stairs, ready to leave.

"Lady Pauline said that everything is ready, Mr. Essex, and in the carriage," the butler told him.

"Thank you, Sedgewick. Is Lady Pauline here?"

"She said she'd see you before you left so she should be here shortly."

"Thank you," Ethan said again, then walked out to the carriage. He looked around but didn't see her, so he took the first step up when a footman opened the door.

He stepped into the carriage, and lifted his head. His gaze locked with hers. "What are you doing in here, Polly?"

"I was waiting for you to arrive. We should be leaving. We won't make it to London before dark if we don't leave soon."

"I want you to stay here. I couldn't live with myself if something happened to you."

"Nothing is going to happen to me," she said.

"You don't know that."

"Yes, I do."

"Sedgewick," Ethan said out of the open door. "Please help Lady Pauline out of the carriage."

"Sedgewick? Who pays your salary?" Polly asked.

"Your father, Lady Pauline," the butler replied.

Ethan closed his eyes in frustration.

"Matter closed," Polly said, obviously trying to keep the smug expression off her face. "Tell the driver we're ready."

"Very well, Lady Pauline."

He did, and the carriage began to move slowly down the tree-lined drive.

It was several miles before Ethan was calm enough to speak to her, but by the time they reached London, he'd had enough laudanum that he was in a much better mood. Polly tried to keep her smugness at bay until they reached Buckingham and were in front of the queen.

CHAPTER FIFTEEN

"HER MAJESTY INSTRUCTED her guards to show you to her private quarters," Lord Springdale said when he stepped into the carriage. "She was adamant that no one connected with the Finance Committee, or with her private staff, sees you."

"Is there a reason for that?" Ethan asked.

"Yes. Her Majesty and I have reached the conclusion that the assassin connected with your injuries is somehow connected to her."

"Do you have any idea who it might be?" Ethan asked.

"No one I can identify with surety."

The carriage traveled the length of the castle, and finally came to a halt in a secluded area.

"Do you know where we are, Ethan?" Polly asked.

"No, I don't. I've never been to this part of the castle."

"Hardly anyone has," her father said.

They entered a gated area, and the carriage stopped. Several guards surrounded the carriage and escorted Polly, Ethan, and Lord Springdale through a door, down a darkened hallway, then through another door. The second door opened to an area made up of several sitting rooms, a dining area, several bedrooms, and a number of other rooms that were a puzzle to Ethan.

Polly led him to one of the sitting rooms and helped him sit. He'd never been more thankful for a chair in his life. Although the carriage had been made as comfortable as possible, the bumps and ruts in the road still took a toll on his body. He hurt in places he hadn't hurt before. To his surprise, walking had been more of a challenge than he could have anticipated.

"I'm going to ask for something for the pain," Polly said when Ethan released a heavy sigh as he sat. "As soon as you've spoken to Her Majesty, I'll get you into bed and you can relax."

"The staff can help Essex to a bed now," her father told Polly as he handed her a small vial. "Her Majesty said she would give Essex several hours to rest before she came to see him. That is to let him recover from the trip and to avoid having anyone follow her."

"Very wise," Polly said, then added some laudanum to a glass of wine. When she had it mixed, she handed it to Ethan and let him drink.

He took far more than he intended, but he needed the elixir more now than he had before.

"I'm going to rest now," he said, accepting the help to rise and move to the bedroom. Polly followed him into the adjoining room and helped him into the bed. "Polly, mind your father. Don't anger him overmuch. He doesn't like it when you pay too much attention to me."

"I know," she whispered. "But I want him to get used to the idea of us being together."

"But perhaps now is not the time."

She looked at him, and he saw the determination on her face, then the resolve. "Perhaps you are correct. I will try to be more considerate of his feelings. For now."

Ethan smiled. "That's my girl."

She stepped closer to the bed and leaned down to kiss him, and he returned the kiss because he needed her to be close to him. "Sleep well. I'll wake you when Her Majesty arrives."

"Yes. That would be good."

Polly stepped out of the room and closed the door behind her.

POLLY KNEW THAT she and her father were going to have an argument the moment she stepped into the sitting room and saw the scowl on her father's face.

"How often do I have to warn you about fraternizing with a commoner, Pauline?"

"How often do I have to remind you that your words will not affect me when it comes to Ethan?"

"Are you forming a friendship with him only to spite me, daughter? I can't believe you don't realize the differences in your positions. I can't believe you can't see that you will never suit."

"Why won't we suit, Father? Do you consider him that far beneath you that you think he is insignificant?"

"Of course he is beneath me. He is beneath you. You can't even compare the differences."

"Oh, Father," Polly said. "Don't you realize that he's an agent of our queen? That he was the one she asked to help her when she discovered someone had stolen from her? That when you were accused of the crime, Her Majesty was prepared to sacrifice your life, but it was Ethan, the commoner, who bargained with her to allow him to make sure you were guilty before he killed you?"

"But that was no doubt because he knew you would hate him if he killed your father."

"Do you think he's not proficient enough to have eliminated you without my ever knowing?"

Her words shocked him. He clearly hadn't thought of such a plan.

"And do you think he didn't know it would be a thousand times better if he had eliminated you so nothing obstructed his path to possessing me?"

"You would have allowed him to trick you into falling in love with him?"

"I have already fallen in love with him, Father, and there was no trickery involved in how I feel."

"I don't believe this," the marquess said. "This isn't how you were raised. You were raised to know your place and to be an example for the rest of Society. You were not raised to work in a bookshop for the rest of your life and be ignored by Society."

"Perhaps I don't agree with the way I was raised," Polly said, and knew there was nothing more she could say to her father to convince him that Ethan was far and above any man she had ever met. That he was even better. "I think I will rest a few moments before the queen comes. I will also have some tea prepared."

Polly left the room and waited for the queen to arrive. Nothing had been solved with their conversation. Nothing ever would. Her father had no intention of changing his mind.

And she had no intention of giving up Ethan.

ETHAN HEARD THE queen's carriage arrive and threw the covers back. He struggled to get out of bed but needed help. Just then, Polly entered the room and helped him to his feet.

A servant entered the room at the same time to help him dress and put on a fresh cravat.

"Do you want any laudanum? Just enough to ease the pain?" she asked.

Ethan shook his head. "I need a clear head. Laudanum makes my mind fuzzy."

"Is there anything you need me to do or say?" she asked.

"Just remember everything Her Majesty says. I want to make sure we can discuss what she knows after she leaves."

"Perhaps I'll take notes."

"That would be perfect."

"I'll get my sketchpad."

Ethan nodded.

The valet opened the door for Ethan, and he walked into the sitting room. Polly followed behind him then stopped when she came face to face with the queen.

This was the first time Polly had been in the presence of Her Majesty, and she curtsied deeply as she'd been taught, never thinking she'd actually have to use it before the queen.

Ethan bowed as deeply as his injury allowed.

"Help Essex to a chair," Her Majesty ordered one of the footmen who had accompanied her.

"Would you care for something to drink, Your Majesty?" Ethan asked.

"Yes, Essex. You know what I want."

"Yes, Your Majesty." He looked at the footman who had helped him to a chair. "Two whiskys," Ethan said. "What would you like, my lord?" he asked Polly's father.

"I'll take a whisky, as well."

"Three whiskys, and wine for Lady Pauline." While the footman poured their drinks, Ethan looked at the queen. "Allow me to present Lady Pauline, Your Majesty. She is Lord Springdale's daughter and has been invaluable to me."

"I see," the queen said, as if reading more into those few words than Ethan intended.

The footman handed out the whiskys and wine.

"How are you, Essex?" she asked.

"Our killer didn't intend for me to live, but I will have a surprise for him when he sees me."

"You do know that I would have been extremely vexed if you had allowed him to kill you," she said.

"That was in the back of my mind the entire time I was recovering."

"Make sure you don't forget it."

"I won't, Your Majesty. Now, Lord Springdale tells me that you might have a hint as to the identity of our assassin?"

"Let's say I can tell you who he is not."

"That is helpful," Ethan said.

"It's not anyone on the Finance Committee. I can guarantee you that."

"I see," Ethan said. "Then who do you think it is?"

"I believe it is one of my senior palace staff."

"How many staff members are we talking about?"

"Thirty-six," she answered.

"Do any of them stand out to you?"

"I have put four of them on a list. Roger Links, Jeremy Knobes, Clive Oberman, and Harvey Rakes."

Ethan considered the names. "What about the man I met when I called on you that first time?"

"Rupert Blackheart?" she asked. The queen shook her head. "No, he's one of my most trusted advisors. He's as timid as a mouse. He would never steal from me, or harm you. I doubt the poor man has ever fired a pistol, let alone shot at someone with one."

"If you say so," he replied, but looked at Polly with a glance that told her to write Rupert's name down with the other suspects.

"So, how are you going to handle this, Essex?"

"I'm not sure yet. I think my first move will be to let the suspects see me so they know their plot to kill me has failed. Hopefully, that will force them to panic and start to move the stolen money from its hiding place."

"Excellent," the queen said. "That sounds like an excellent plan."

"I hope so."

Her Majesty rose from her chair, and everyone stood. "I'll send food to you. I doubt you have had dinner as of yet, have you?"

"No, Your Majesty. A hearty meal would be most welcome."

Queen Victoria nodded, then turned toward the door. "Someone will be here soon with food. Write instructions for tomorrow and send them with one of the servants. Instruct them to keep your presence a secret."

"Yes, Your Majesty. We will formulate our plans yet tonight and send them to you first thing in the morning."

She nodded, then walked out the door. Everyone stood where they had been for several long minutes before any of them moved.

"Come, Pauline," the Marquess of Springdale said. "Allow me to escort you to the dining room. Her Majesty said our food would be here shortly."

"Are you coming, Ethan?" Polly asked him, but Ethan remained quiet for a moment and did nothing except smile. Polly's father was making it as plain as he could that Ethan was not welcome to eat with them. He was silently making it clear that the difference in their stations was too great a chasm to cross.

"I might eat in my room. Go on and dine without me."

Ethan sat in his chair for a little while, then rose and went to his room. He instructed a footman to fix him a plate when the food arrived, then he poured some wine into a glass and added a small amount of laudanum to it.

He knew he would need it to not only to dull the pain that threatened to overtake him, but to dull his emotions. His need for Polly was intense, made even worse by the fact that her father intended to do everything in his power to keep Ethan from having her.

Chapter Sixteen

POLLY FILLED A plate with food for Ethan and, after her father retired for the evening, took it to his room. She hoped he would still be awake, but he wasn't. Instead of leaving like she knew she should, she covered the food to help it stay warm then sat down in a chair and watched him.

He was the most handsome man she'd ever seen, and she loved him more than she ever thought she would love anyone. She always knew that someday she would marry. But she thought the man she married would be someone her father had chosen for her. It would be an arranged marriage, not a marriage based on love. She'd never expected to love the man she married. But she loved Ethan and couldn't imagine marrying anyone else.

She focused on his face, and his startling blue eyes looked back at her.

"How long have you been sitting there?" he asked.

"Not long. How do you feel?"

"Better. The ride here wore me out."

"I was afraid it would. We should have let you heal more before you attempted to travel."

"That wasn't possible. We had to get here before our thief gathered his stolen money and left with it."

"Is that what you think he will do?"

Ethan nodded, then swung his legs over the side of the bed

and held out his hand for Polly to help him sit. When he was upright, he reached for the glass of wine and laudanum. "Did you bring the notes you took?" he asked, then took a swallow from his glass.

"Yes. Drink a little more wine and I'll get your plate ready."

Ethan looked at the food Polly was putting on his plate and held up a hand. "That is plenty," he said when he saw how much she was giving him. "I'm not that hungry."

"I know you're not, but you have to eat. You need the nourishment."

He smiled at her and took the plate while she slid a small table in front of him. "Read the notes you took while I eat."

Polly read the notes to him, then stopped when she got to the name Ethan had her add, even though Her Majesty didn't think he was a possibility.

"Who is Rupert Blackheart?" she asked.

"He's one of Her Majesty's most trusted advisors. He knows more about her business than she does. I've only met him a few times, but I don't like him."

"You don't like him?"

"No. He's too inquisitive. He's a plotter. He's one of those people who plays dumb but isn't. Instead, he's sly as a fox. He's a conniver."

"I see," Polly said, knowing if Ethan didn't trust this man, she shouldn't either.

"You don't trust my instincts, do you?"

"Just the opposite, Ethan. I don't understand them, but I trust them. Now, finish your dinner so we can figure out what to do first. Should we work our way through the committee members? Or should we concentrate on this Blackheart?"

"What do you think?" Ethan asked.

"Do you think Blackheart is his real name?"

"No," Ethan answered. "I think it's a name he chose to add to his false identity."

"Oh," Polly said, wondering why anyone would do that.

Unless they wanted to build a wall around themselves. "I think we should concentrate on him first."

"Good idea," Ethan said, smiling. "Why do you think that?"

"Because if this Blackheart is the man who tried to kill you, we don't want to tip him off because we were concentrating on everyone else first. We need to arrest him before he has time to draw the money he stole out of whatever bank he hid it in."

"You are very smart for a Society miss," he said. "You could be a thief."

"I don't want to be a thief. I just want this to be over so we can get back to Willowbrook and resume our lives."

"Me too," he said.

Polly took Ethan's plate and set it on the table, then sat down beside him on the bed. He wrapped his arm around her, and she leaned her head on his uninjured shoulder.

Ethan kissed her forehead, then lowered his mouth to her lips. He kissed her several times and didn't stop until he could no longer breathe. "Has your father gone to bed?" he asked when he broke off their kiss.

"I think so, but I'm not sure."

"I don't want him to find us like this. He's angry enough at us without walking in on us kissing each other."

"That does fire him up, doesn't it?" Polly said on a laugh.

"I don't know how you can find that humorous, Polly."

"Probably because I've already made my choice."

"What choice?"

"My choice between you and my father."

"And your choice is?"

"You, Ethan. It was always you. Now Father is the only one who has to make a choice—between accepting you and me together, or his being alone. If he wants to be alone for the rest of his life, that will be his choice."

"Oh, Polly. Do you know what you're saying?"

"Yes, I know. But I can't give you up. I can't."

"I love you, Polly. You are the other half of my heart, the half that shares its beats with mine."

Ethan turned his head and pressed his lips to hers. Thankfully, their kiss had just ended when the door opened and the Marquess of Springdale entered the room.

"Pauline! Leave here this instant!"

Polly slid over so there was room separating them. "No, Father. We think we know who framed you and who shot Ethan."

The marquess stopped his rant and focused on Ethan. "Are you certain?"

"As certain as we can be at this point."

The marquess asked Ethan, "Who? Who do you think it is?"

"Blackheart."

"Blackheart? It can't be. He's a fool! Why Her Majesty trusts him, I don't know. He's a buffoon!"

"That's what he would like everyone to think. That he's the court jester. But he's not. He's actually a manipulator."

"How will we know if he's the guilty one?"

"We'll let him tell us," Ethan said.

"How?"

"Do you know Her Majesty's schedule for the remainder of the week?"

"No, but I can find out what it is."

"Then do it. We'll need to know her schedule for tomorrow and the next four or five days. And we'll want Her Majesty to witness his betrayal so she has absolute proof."

"I'll go in the morning to ask for an audience with the queen," the marquess said. "Then I'll ask for her schedule for the remainder of this week."

"We'll pick a time that will work the best, then you will ask to meet with her in private. She will, of course, take one senior advisor with her to take notes of your meeting. She will no doubt choose Blackheart, as he is the advisor she relies on the most. If she doesn't choose him, you'll have to suggest him."

"She'll choose Blackheart. I have no doubt of that."

Ethan thought the same. "This will be the most sensitive part of our plan. You'll need to convince Her Majesty that you've discovered some discrepancies within the Finance Committee's books. A sizeable amount lost."

"But she already knows about that," Lord Springdale said.

"Yes, but she won't expect you to bring the matter to her attention. Neither will Blackheart. It will surprise him."

"The queen will no doubt ask you if you know the identity of the thief. You will tell her that you don't know who he is for certain, but you promise to get to the bottom of the matter."

"Then what?" Lord Springdale asked.

"If at all possible, you'll wait outside the door and see if you can hear what Blackheart and the queen discuss inside."

"If I can't?"

"Return here. I'll try to follow Blackheart when he leaves and see where he goes."

"No," Polly interrupted. "In the first place, you can't risk being seen. Blackheart will recognize you. I will follow him. He doesn't know me. I'll see where he goes."

"I don't want you involved in this, Polly," Ethan replied. "It could be dangerous."

"No, Ethan. What is dangerous about a woman walking the streets of London? I'll be careful."

"I don't like it either," Lord Springdale said. "But what choice do we have? Someone needs to follow him so we know which bank he goes to. It's the only way we'll know where he has some of the money deposited."

Ethan didn't like it, but Polly was correct—Blackheart recognizing Ethan would ruin the entire plan, and they'd never be able to prove the marquess innocent.

"Very well," he said. "But I still don't like it."

Polly smiled at him, then reached for his hand and squeezed his fingers.

"Is there anything else?" Lord Springdale asked.

"All we need to do tomorrow is follow him when he goes to

the bank. We will complete our trap the next day when Her Majesty can witness everything."

"Very well," the marquess agreed, then turned his focus to Polly. "You need to go to your room, and stay there," he ordered her.

"Yes, Father."

Polly rose and left the room, but first she reached for Ethan's hand and gave his fingers another gentle squeeze. Her father followed her out of the room.

Ethan thought for sure Polly's father would issue him a warning about staying away from his daughter, but he didn't. Ethan was surprised, but knew it wasn't over.

⊱❋⊰

ETHAN, POLLY, AND Lord Springdale went through their plan again before Polly and her father left.

Ethan tried to relax while they were gone, but that was impossible. He couldn't help but play the scenes over in his mind. He couldn't help but imagine what would happen if the queen refused to allow Blackheart to accompany her into her meeting with Springdale.

There were so many things that could go wrong. But most of all, he worried about Polly. What if Blackheart recognized her? What if he realized she was following him? What if he attacked her? What if he harmed her?

He paced the floor from one window to the other. He poured himself a glass of whisky and took a sip, then set it down. Dulling his senses wouldn't do anyone any good. He needed to stay sharp. He needed to remain alert in case Polly needed him.

He walked the floor again, and this time his steps were answered by a sound at the door. He turned to see the smiling face of the Marquess of Springdale.

"Your plan went off like clockwork."

Ethan breathed a sigh of relief.

"I asked to see Her Majesty and told her it was important. She motioned for Blackheart to accompany her, and we went into a private room. I explained that I had found some irregularities in the books and was afraid someone was stealing from the Finance Committee. She asked if I knew who, and I said I didn't yet, but I intended to find out. She thanked me for my diligence and dismissed me.

"I left and waited as long as I thought was safe. Just as I was going to leave, Blackheart left Buckingham and took the side entrance out of the building."

"Did you see your daughter?" Ethan asked.

"No, but I'm sure she was there. That's the exit I told her to watch."

Ethan nodded, then looked at the mantel clock. If nothing went wrong, she should be here soon.

But she didn't come.

They waited longer, and still she didn't arrive.

"Sit down, Essex," Polly's father told him. "You're making me nervous."

"It shouldn't take her this long. She should be back by now."

"You obviously haven't had to wait on many women before. They can take longer to look at items in just a shop window than it takes for men to purchase every item in the entire place."

Thankfully, just then the door opened and Polly entered the room.

Ethan turned, then took three long steps toward the door and pulled her into his arms. "Are you all right?"

"Of course I am, you worrier," she replied.

"Did you see where he went?" her father asked her, forcing her to turn out of Ethan's arms.

"He went to Barclays."

"We've got him," Ethan said.

CHAPTER SEVENTEEN

"Y OU HAVE A guest, Your Majesty," the doorman announced, opening the door to the sitting room where the queen worked behind her desk.

She looked up, and so did every other person in the room.

The Marquess of Springdale entered the room first, and Ethan entered next. Ethan bowed to Her Majesty, then took his first steps to stand before Rupert Blackheart.

Blackheart lifted his head, and his jaw dropped. "Mr. Essex," he stammered through his hoarse throat.

"What?" Ethan asked. "Are you surprised to see me?"

"I… uh… I… No, of course not. Not really."

"I think you are, Blackheart. I don't think you expected to see me alive ever again."

"What is Essex saying, Blackheart?" Her Majesty asked, rising from behind her desk.

"Why don't you tell her, Blackheart? Tell her why you didn't think you'd ever see me again?"

"I don't know what you are talking about, Essex," Blackheart replied.

"I am saying that you didn't think you would ever see me again because you thought you had killed me."

"What? You don't know what you're saying."

"But I do. I know that you shot me three times and thought I was dead. But I wasn't. I only pretended that I was. And even then, you came over to me and kicked me in the ribs to make sure I was dead."

"Blackheart," the queen said. "Is this true?"

"Of course not, Your Majesty. Essex is lying. He's never liked me. He's always been jealous of me and is trying to sully my name and reputation."

"Your Majesty," Ethan said, "I would like you to look at Blackheart's shoes. If he is wearing the same shoes he wore when he tried to kill me, the right side of his right shoe will be scuffed."

"Show me your shoe, Blackheart," the queen said.

"That doesn't mean anything, Your Majesty," Blackheart replied. "The polish is worn on several of your agents' shoes. That happens from sitting at a desk for several hours a day."

Her Majesty focused on Ethan again.

"That may be true, Your Majesty," Ethan said, "but not every one of your agents has bank accounts at Barclays with such an astronomical amount in it as Mr. Blackheart does."

Lord Springdale pulled a piece of paper from his breast pocket and walked to the queen who sat at the desk.

Without warning, Blackheart pulled a gun from a drawer in the credenza and aimed it at Springdale.

Ethan wasn't sure where the bullet was going to go. The most likely person and greatest casualty would be the queen.

He leaped toward her, knowing that he was going to take another bullet for queen and country. He prayed he could survive this one the same as he'd survived the last three.

He knocked Springdale out of the way as he hurdled the desk and wrapped his arms around Queen Victoria.

Blackheart's gun fired, and Ethan experienced a fiery pain at his waist. Before Blackheart was able to fire another shot, the door flew open. Her Majesty's guards rushed into the room with their weapons drawn and sent bullets spraying toward Rupert Blackheart.

"Ethan!" Polly's voice sounded from the door.

Several guards rushed to where the queen lay on the floor with Ethan covering her. They lifted him off her, then gently assisted Her Majesty to her feet.

"Call for my physician," she said.

"Where are you hurt, Your Majesty?" several guards yelled out.

"It's not for me. I'm not hurt. Mr. Essex needs the physician. He's been injured."

Several guards carried Ethan to Her Majesty's private sitting room and placed him on a bed. Polly went with him.

"How badly are you hurt?" she asked.

"I'm not sure," he gasped. "I don't think badly at all. I'm still quite sore from before."

"Of course." Polly turned to the door. "The physician is here."

"Don't let him bleed me, Polly. Promise me."

"I promise."

"How is he, doctor?" the queen asked.

The physician removed Ethan's shirt and examined the wound that was still bleeding at his waist. "He should be dead," the doctor said, checking the wounds from when Blackheart shot Ethan the first time. "How long ago were these sustained?"

"Several weeks ago," Polly replied.

"I was going to suggest we bleed you, but you've lost so much blood already it would be pointless."

"Quite," Ethan said.

"The wound you sustained today is less damaging. It just needs to be cleaned and stitched. It should heal on its own. I'll rebandage the chest wound. It's bleeding again, and that's not good."

"Will he be all right?" the queen asked.

"He'll heal well enough in time, Your Majesty. I'd suggest that he doesn't let anyone else use him for target practice for the next thirty or forty years, however."

"He won't," Polly said, swiping a tear from her eye. "We'll

take him home and he can do what he does best."

"And what is that?" Her Majesty asked.

"Run his bookshop and write children's books. He's remarkably gifted at both."

"I would never have guessed," the queen said with a startled expression.

"Just as no one would guess that he's an agent for the Crown," Polly replied.

"Very true," the queen responded. "Are you finished?" she asked the physician.

"Yes, Your Majesty. I don't believe I can do any more damage. He seems to do enough of that on his own."

"Yes, he does."

"He's asleep now and should remain so for several hours. I gave him enough laudanum to keep him out of pain until he wakes."

"Good. Anything else?"

"I wouldn't advise any traveling for at least a week."

"Did you hear that, Lord Springdale?" she asked.

"Yes, Your Majesty," the marquess replied. "If we might impose upon your hospitality that long?"

"Of course you may. I am unharmed because of Mr. Essex. It is the very least I can do." Queen Victoria turned to Polly. "I assume you will stay with Essex until he wakes, Lady Pauline?"

"Of course, Your Majesty," Polly said as she curtsied.

The queen walked to the door, then stopped when a guard opened it. "I will expect to see you tomorrow, Lord Springdale. I have several questions that beg to be answered."

"By all means, Your Majesty," the marquess said.

"I presume any traces of this travesty have been removed from my office?" she asked the guard.

"Completely, Your Majesty."

"And the Resolute? It is untarnished?"

"Your desk remains unscathed, Your Majesty."

Queen Victoria looked relieved as she passed the senior

guard.

The door closed, and Polly could hear no more. "Are you going to stay here, Papa, or return to our quarters?"

"There's no need for me to stay here," her father replied. "The physician said he's given Essex enough laudanum to keep him asleep until morning. I still think it's unseemly for you to stay with him. Her Majesty should have thought better before she ordered you to nurse Essex."

"I would have stayed here anyway," Polly said. She wanted her father to know how determined she was to be with Ethan.

Her father simply shook his head and walked out the door.

⤜⤜⤜※⤛⤛⤛

ETHAN WOKE THE next morning with a mouth full of cotton and an anvil pounding in his head. "What did that physician give me yesterday? I hurt like hell."

"I think he gave you an extra amount of laudanum," Polly answered.

He turned his head and tried to focus on her, but there were three of her and he didn't know which one was the real Polly.

"What are you doing here?"

"The queen ordered me to stay with you."

"She what?"

"She ordered me to stay with you."

"And your father allowed it?"

"I don't think even Father would be brave enough to argue with the queen."

"I would have."

"Yes, I believe you would have. Especially if you were in the mood you are this morning."

Ethan breathed a deep sigh. "I'm sorry, Polly. Would you find me a cup of coffee?"

"I have one right here. Do you want me to add a little laudanum to it?"

"No. I don't want to add to my problem. I just want a dozen cups of black coffee."

"A dozen?" Polly said on a laugh.

"Maybe two."

"Well, here's number one," she said, then handed him a cup of hot coffee. "Be careful, it's—"

"Hot!" he bellowed.

"Yes, it's hot."

Ethan blew on the liquid in his cup, then took another sip. "Better," he said. "What instructions did Her Majesty leave with you?"

"Other than that I was supposed to stay with you, she said she wanted to see us sometime today."

"I don't doubt that. She probably still can't believe Blackheart was the thief, or that he would have killed her if I hadn't jumped in front of her."

"Do you really think he intended to kill her?"

Ethan shook his head. "No, I think he intended to kill your father."

"Father? Why?"

"With your father dead, he could have tried to convince the queen that your father had lied about everything, then showed a deposit amount from the Barclay bank that was really your father's and not his."

"Do you think Her Majesty would have believed it?"

"With the marquess dead, and me as well, who could tell her the truth?"

"He would have killed you, too?"

"He'd tried and failed enough times."

"Father is very lucky you were here to save him."

"Yes," Ethan said, then finished his coffee.

Polly lifted the silver urn and refilled his cup. "Better?"

"Yes. And it's not quite as hot."

"How's your head?"

"Better, but it still hurts."

"I imagine it does. I can't believe how quickly you went to sleep. I looked over at you and you were awake. The next second I looked, you were asleep."

"Whatever that physician gave me knocked me out fast."

Before Ethan could finish the next cup of coffee, the door opened and Polly's father entered the room.

"Good morning," he said cheerfully.

"Good morning, Papa," she replied.

"Lord Springdale," Ethan greeted him.

"Did you receive the message from the queen?" the marquess asked.

Polly looked at Ethan, and they both shook their heads.

"What does she want?" Ethan asked.

"She wishes to meet with us. She's sending a light lunch and wants us to give a full explanation of everything."

"I expected her to want to know everything we discovered and how we figured out Blackheart was the thief," Ethan said. "She loathes unanswered questions."

"Well, there are several in this case."

"Yes, there are."

As they spoke, a knock sounded at the door and several maids entered with a tea cart and another cart laden with pastries.

"Oh my," Polly said, looking at the pastries. "The kitchen must have been up all night baking."

"No doubt," Lord Springdale agreed.

He'd barely finished his sentence when the door opened again and Her Majesty entered, followed by three servants carrying cushioned chairs. Lord Springdale bowed, and Polly curtsied, but when Ethan struggled to stand, the queen held out her hand and motioned for him to remain in bed.

"We will enjoy a cup of tea first," Her Majesty said as the servants poured and served the tea. Then another maid carried the pastries around, so everyone had something to eat. While they drank their tea and ate their pastries, the queen kept the conversation light.

She asked several questions about Willowbrook and how fast the town was growing. She asked what shops were opening and which ones they would like to see go in.

Then she asked Ethan how he was feeling, and, of course, he said he was well and would be up and around in no time. He also apologized for his slowness, but he'd not fully recovered as of yet.

When they were finished with their pastries, she motioned for the maids to collect the dishes and leave. Everyone was silent until all that remained were Lord Springdale, Polly, Ethan, the queen, and one of her advisors who was there to take notes.

"Now, Mr. Essex, I want to hear exactly what happened, and don't leave anything out."

"Yes, Your Majesty," Ethan replied.

"And I want to know how you came to the conclusion that Lord Springdale is innocent, and your reason had better be more than the fact that you are in love with his daughter."

Ethan swallowed past the lump in his throat. "Yes, Your Majesty."

CHAPTER EIGHTEEN

ETHAN TOOK A deep breath before he started. "As you know, you asked to see me concerning a substantial amount of money you were told was missing from the Finance Committee accounts."

"Yes, it amounted to one hundred thousand pounds," the queen replied.

"Yes. You informed me that you had been told that the Marquess of Springdale was behind the theft."

"And what were your instructions?"

"I was to eliminate the thief, but you didn't want anyone to know the reason for his death. You wanted it to look like a robbery."

"And the reason I wanted this?"

Ethan glanced at Polly, wishing he could spare her a rehashing of these uncomfortable details. But the queen was adamant that he was not to dodge the truth.

"You knew he had a daughter, and you didn't want Society to know that her father was a thief. You wanted to spare her the embarrassment of a public hanging."

"Yes." Her Majesty turned to the man taking notes. "Are you getting all this?"

"Yes, Your Majesty."

"You'd better. I need a complete accounting. Go on, Essex."

"On the ride home, I went over everything in my mind and came to the conclusion that Lord Springdale's guilt was nothing but hearsay," Ethan continued. "I needed proof."

"And you came to that conclusion on your own?" the queen asked. "Are you saying that it had nothing to do with your feelings for Lady Pauline?"

"Well, it could not have, Your Majesty. You see, I had not met the dear lady at that point. Even so, I would say no. I did meet her shortly after, however, and that merely affirmed my need to ferret out the truth. I began to feel that because of the kind of person Lady Pauline is—honest, forthright, intelligent, and trustworthy—she must have been raised by someone who lived by those same values."

"Go on. You needed proof. Did you find any?"

"I did. I managed to break into Lord Springdale's mansion several nights. Because he is such a meticulous person, I thought it was quite likely that he would keep a record of the exact amount of money he'd embezzled, and what the total was."

"Did you find a record?" the queen asked.

"Yes. It was written in a ledger, but I almost didn't discover the secret ledger. It was hidden in a wall safe behind several books in a bookcase. Unfortunately, I hadn't discovered the combination of the safe when Lady Pauline caught me going through her father's study.

"She demanded to know what I was doing, and I saw no need not to tell her, so I did. She told me I wouldn't find anything in the safe because her father wasn't guilty. She was certain that he wasn't."

"How did you get the safe open?"

"Lady Pauline knew the combination and opened it for me," Ethan said. "She was eager to prove her father's innocence and was convinced that I wouldn't find anything. I took out the ledger that was in the safe, and on the last page, I found a list of all of the transactions, including the amounts taken from the Finance Committee."

"What did you do then?" Her Majesty asked.

"I informed Lady Pauline that I didn't have a choice. My assignment was to kill her father, and that's what I had to do. But I felt I needed more. Even a confession, if that were possible. When I challenged the marquess with our evidence, he pointed out several discrepancies in the handwriting. Upon close investigation, we determined that the last page in the ledger—the page with the most damning evidence—was a forgery. That's when I went to tell you." Ethan took a deep breath.

"Continue, Essex," Queen Victoria said.

"On my way back to Willowbrook, I was shot. Blackheart shot me three times. I didn't know who it was at first, but after he shot me, he walked up to me and kicked me in the ribs. When he approached me, I got a look at his shoes. They weren't Lord Springdale's shoes. These shoes were scuffed. Springdale would never wear scuffed shoes, and his trousers were frayed at the cuff. That's when I knew Springdale was innocent."

Ethan stopped to rest. He was getting tired.

"Would you like something to drink?" Her Majesty asked.

"I would appreciate something."

"Humphries, call for a footman."

"Yes, Your Majesty." The secretary placed his paper on the chair and opened the door to get someone's attention.

"A drop of whisky in red wine, if you please," she said, requesting one of her preferred libations. "And Essex will take whisky." She turned to Lord Springdale.

"The same," he said.

"Just wine, please," Polly said when the queen looked at her.

They were all served, then Ethan and the marquess were given more whisky.

When the secretary sat back in his chair, the queen looked at Ethan. "Continue, Mr. Essex."

"I don't remember much of what happened after that, Your Majesty. I somehow managed to get back on my horse and rode it toward Springdale's manor house. Thankfully, my horse stopped in the drive, and I fell off. The stable hands found me, and Lady Pauline took me in and called for a doctor. The rest you know."

"No, Essex. I'd like to know how you narrowed the suspects to Rupert Blackheart."

"Oh, yes. That took a little detective work. We had to rely on the fact that Blackheart thought I was dead. Lord Springdale went to see you. He informed you that he'd found a discrepancy in the Finance Committee ledgers. Once Blackheart found out Springdale knew about the missing money, he'd know it was only a matter of time until we realized who was stealing from the committee. That was when we had him followed."

"Followed where?"

"To Barclays to withdraw his money. That was Lady Pauline's role. She was to follow him to determine where he stored his money. There are more banks in this area than one realizes."

"That was where you got the paper stating the amount of money in Blackheart's account," the queen said.

Ethan struggled not to meet her pointed gaze.

"What?" she asked. "What are you not telling me?"

"We didn't exactly have a paper that said the amount of money Blackheart had in his account."

"What was the paper you handed me?"

"A blank piece of paper. A piece of paper that displayed a Barclays letterhead. A piece of paper that Blackheart would assume could indict him."

"Awfully risky, Essex."

"But it worked. That's exactly what Blackheart thought it was."

"Yes." Her Majesty drained her glass, then looked at Ethan. "Are you sure I cannot change your mind about leaving my force?"

"No, Your Majesty. I am quite determined. The bullets I took in this last assignment convinced me that if I remain in your service, I will probably end up dead."

The queen lifted her brows. "You are probably right," she said, "and that would be a shame."

"Thank you, Your Majesty."

"I will expect you to remain as my guest for what is left of the week. The physician tells me you have improved greatly, but you are not ready to travel yet. I don't want you to travel too soon."

"Thank you, Your Majesty.

"I also wish you the best success with your shop. The Page Turner Bookshop, isn't it?"

"Yes, Your Majesty."

"If there is anything I can do for you, Ethan, don't hesitate to ask."

"Thank you, Your Majesty," Ethan said, then bowed.

He watched the queen leave the room and was surprised when Lord Springdale followed. He must have something important to discuss with her privately. Perhaps something concerning the Finance Committee and the loss of such a sum of money.

Ethan turned and stared at Polly.

"She is fond of you, Ethan," she said with flushed cheeks. "She speaks very highly of you, and I truly believe she will miss having you in her corner."

"And I will miss her," Ethan admitted. "She has a curt manner about her, and it's difficult to understand her reasoning at times, but she is loyal to Britain and will do anything for her country."

"She is not at all like I imagined her to be," Polly said.

"Do you mean she is by far too short in stature and too plump to be regal, and she's not above mixing whisky in her wine, and she more often than not doesn't stop at one glass?"

"You summed her up to perfection," Polly replied. "But I believe she has a sharp mind and is no fool."

"In that you are correct," Ethan said, then stepped closer to her. "What do you think your father is discussing with her?"

"I have no idea. He didn't mention anything to me about a matter he wanted to speak to the queen about."

"It must be nothing," Ethan said, but he knew it wasn't "nothing." It was "something," and whatever it was, he doubted he would like it.

⋙✠⋘

"YES, SPRINGDALE," THE queen said. "You have something that demands my attention?"

"Yes, Your Majesty. It concerns my daughter."

"Your daughter?"

"Yes. As I'm sure you have noticed, she is of marriageable age, and is pleasing to look at."

"She is beautiful. She will be a diamond of the first water when she has her Season. Why is it that she has not had her first?"

"She refused to have a Season," Lord Springdale replied. "She has this strange opinion that being put on the Marriage Mart is nothing more than being a horse on sale to the highest bidder. She insists that she will marry for love and not to enhance family connections."

"I see," the queen said on a laugh. "But you do not agree?"

"I want her to make an enviable match. I want her to marry into a fine family and take her rightful place in Society."

"What about her desire for love? Is that not important to you?"

"It is very important. Pauline's mother and I loved each other very much in the end."

"But not when you married?"

"Love grew in our marriage, as I am certain it will in Pauline's."

"But what about her love for Ethan Essex?" Her Majesty asked. "You *can* see that they are in love, can't you?"

"That is the reason I am speaking to you. She only thinks she loves Essex. But that love will fade in time. He has nothing to offer her. He will do nothing for her but bring her down in

Society's eyes. She will forever be nothing more than the wife of a commoner. A shopkeeper's wife! Bloody hell. Essex doesn't even own a home. Where would they live? Essex lives above his shop."

"That does not please you?"

"Of course it doesn't please me. Pauline can do so much better."

"Yes, I truly believe she can." Her Majesty paused a moment. "So, what exactly are you asking of me, Lord Springdale?"

"I would like your assistance in finding Pauline an enviable match. Someone high enough in rank and financial status that she can take her rightful place in Society."

"I see," the queen said thoughtfully. "Yes, I believe I can do that. For the role you played in uncovering the thief who intended to steal from me, I can do that."

"Thank you, Your Majesty. I am forever in your debt."

Lord Springdale bowed to her, then left the room, his mission accomplished.

CHAPTER NINETEEN

EVERYTHING WAS FINALLY back to normal. Ethan was healed and back working in his bookshop. Polly had been working on the illustrations for another children's book he'd written, and his father was still in Willowbrook enjoying a few days with Ethan. They weren't sure when they'd see each other again.

Ethan felt as if the last few months had been a dream—or more like a nightmare. He was glad the nightmare was over and he could be back to doing what he loved.

He was working in his bookshop one beautiful afternoon when a rider approached. The man's livery startled Ethan. This was an emissary from the queen. Ethan bristled. He'd made it clear he was no longer willing to serve at her bidding. What could she want with him? She knew there would be no more killing. No more spying. No more espionage.

Ethan stepped out onto the walkway in front of his shop. "Were you sent by the queen?"

"Yes, sir. Her Majesty requests your presence at the home of Lord Springdale."

"The queen is here?"

"Yes, sir."

"Did she give a reason for requesting my presence?"

"No, sir. I am only to give you her message."

Ethan turned at the sound of excited chatter behind him.

Along both sides of the street, people were being escorted toward the village center by footmen dressed in the same livery as the emissary standing beside him. The townfolk looked pleased. Excited. The queen's footmen seemed to be treating them kindly.

"Is something wrong?" Ethan's father asked when he came out of the bookshop.

"I don't know. I don't think so, but one never knows. Come, we're to go to Springdale's."

He and his father made their way to Lord Springdale's estate, and Ethan grew nervous when he realized the woman who stood next to Polly was Queen Victoria. He stopped and bowed, then waited until Her Majesty motioned for him to come to her.

Lord Springdale flanked Her Majesty on one side, and Polly stood on the other. Ethan looked at Polly as if she held the answer to what the queen wanted. But her look was equally mystified.

He felt the crowd grow behind him and imagined that the entire town was there. Even Hunter Melbourne, Earl of Murdock, his wife Torie, and their baby son were there. And the Duke of Willowbrook, who had founded the town and built a majority of it, and his wife, the former dowager Countess of Wickham, now the Duchess of Willowbrook, were there. Everyone was there. Even the new doctor, the new librarian, and the vicar. Everyone was excited that Queen Victoria had come to their charming town.

When the crowd noise quieted, Her Majesty stepped to the edge of the portico and looked out on the gathering.

"I know you are all wondering why I am here. I know you want to know what grand event has made me pay a special visit to Willowbrook. There is a twofold reason. The first is to look at your burgeoning city. A city started by the visionary dream of one man. A dream that is now a reality. And that man is the Duke of Willowbrook."

The queen paused while the crowd broke into thunderous applause.

"People like His Grace were the visionaries who forged a path and made our country a great nation."

The crowd raised more applause.

"And it is because of people like Ethan Essex that our nation remains safe."

There was the slight murmuring of questioning confusion.

"None of you are aware of the heroic acts this courageous soldier performed in the line of duty both during the war and after. He is a true example of courage and bravery. But his greatest act of heroism was something he did after the war. A few short weeks ago.

"This amazing deed of bravery is something you will never hear about because he will not tell you. He will not tell you any of his deeds of heroism, but I will. Because of Ethan Essex's bravery, I am alive today. He dove in front of an assassin's bullet to save my life."

A loud gasp erupted from the crowd, followed by cheers and applause.

It took several minutes for the cheering to die down, and the crowd became quiet enough that the queen could be heard.

"This is the kind of bravery that makes our country so great." She turned to Ethan.

Ethan had never wanted any of his acts of heroism to be recognized. He only wanted to be known as a common bookshop owner who lived a quiet life. He never expected to be called to the public's attention by the Queen of England. But here he was, standing in front of the entire citizenry of Willowbrook, being hailed as a hero.

He turned his focus to Polly. She stood in front of him with a look of pride on her face, as if the sun was shining down on just the two of them. Tears of joy spilled across her lashes and ran down her cheeks. The love shining from her eyes was blinding. He loved her more at this point than ever before.

The queen then held up her hand to demand silence. The area became so quiet you could hear the proverbial pin drop.

"Ethan Essex of Willowbrook, I command you to kneel."

Ethan knelt.

The queen took a royal sword that one of the guards handed her and placed the sword on his right shoulder, then his left shoulder, then on his head. "I dub thee Sir Ethan Essex. Rise, Sir Ethan."

He rose on quaking legs, and the crowd raised cheers even louder than before.

The queen held up her hands to demand silence. "In grateful appreciation for your service to our country, I bequeath you the estate formerly known as Palmerton Estate."

The sound heard from the crowd was one of disbelief. Palmerton Estate was one of the most profitable estates in the area. It bordered the land owned by the Duke of Willowbrook and was situated next to Willowbrook Estate. It had been owned by the Crown, but now would be owned by Ethan and Pauline.

"This will go to you as a wedding gift upon your marriage."

Another riotous cheer erupted.

Her Majesty then turned to face the Marquess of Springdale. "Don't you have an announcement to make, Lord Springdale? Your requirements have now been met. Your daughter has a mansion in which to live. A knighted husband to love. And a life of happiness to live."

Polly's father hesitated, then spoke. "Y-yes," he stuttered. "It gives me great pleasure to announce the betrothal of my daughter, Lady Pauline, to Sir Ethan Essex."

Polly met Ethan in front of Her Majesty and wrapped her arms around his neck. He lowered his head and graced his future wife with a kiss as chaste as passion would allow.

The crowd of onlookers bellowed their hearty congratulations. When Ethan and Polly ended their kiss, the Marquess of Springdale approached his daughter and congratulated her, then held out his hand to his future son-in-law to congratulate him. Ethan's father was next to congratulate his son and future daughter-in-law.

When the commotion died down, Ethan and Polly stood together to receive a series of heartfelt congratulations from the townspeople. At the end of the well-wishes, the Duke and Duchess of Willowbrook and Ethan's good friends the Earl and Countess of Murdock approached them to offer their congratulations.

"Oh, am I glad to see you," Ethan said to his best friend, Hunt.

"Do you want to tell me what you want, or do you want me to tell you what you want from me?" Hunt asked.

"You already know, don't you?"

"I know you were raised in the city and don't know the first thing about farming practices or running an estate."

"You always were a genius."

"Perhaps you might join us for dinner some night soon and we can discuss how to alleviate some of your problems."

"That sounds wonderful."

They conversed a while longer, then Ethan and Polly said farewell to the queen, and watched as she left the estate. When she was gone, they walked through the throng of well-wishers and accepted their congratulations. Then they returned to the Page Turner Bookshop and celebrated in private with a glass of brandy.

THE FOLLOWING WEEK, the Duke and Duchess of Willowbrook invited them for a special dinner to celebrate their upcoming nuptials. Everyone was there.

Polly looked around the room and focused on the people who would be her future family. There was Ethan, her future husband. Ethan's father sat with Mrs. Tenpin. The two of them had become quite close, since they'd spent so much time together. And there was her father, who had given up so very much over the past week. He no doubt was still unhappy about being tricked by the queen, forcing him to announce the engagement in front of the entire town of Willowbrook.

Everything her father had always wanted for her was within her grasp, and yet…

None of it was what she truly wanted, except for Ethan. Yes, she wanted him more than anything. He was the only man she ever wanted or would ever love.

"Where will you choose to be married?" Ethan's father asked when he was able to get a word into the conversation.

"In Willowbrook," she answered at the same time her father said, "In London."

There was a pregnant silence.

"I'd like to get married here, Father," she said.

"And I'd like you to be married in London," her father said with emphasis.

Everyone looked at Ethan. "Oh no you don't. I'm not getting involved in this. I am going to get married wherever my bride tells me."

"We'll discuss this later," Lord Springdale said with a false smile on his face.

"I believe," Ethan said with a genuine smile, "that this is the first of many such discussions my future wife and her father will have regarding a variety of subjects."

"Just wait until you are the one she argues with," Polly's father said.

"That will be a rare experience, my lord," Ethan said.

"Are you telling me that you and my daughter don't argue with each other?"

Ethan turned his gaze to Polly. Smiles broke out on their faces. "I have to admit, we rarely disagree on anything. We seem to find agreement on most subjects. I guess our minds just think alike."

Lord Springdale's jaw dropped to his chest. "I don't believe this."

Everyone laughed.

"May I interject a comment here?" Ethan's father said.

"Please," Lord Springdale said.

"May I suggest that the reason you and your daughter find occasion to argue is because your temperaments are very much alike. You each know what you want, but you don't want the same things. Polly and Ethan are the same, yet different. They each know what they want, but what they want happens to be the same thing."

"Yes, Mr. Essex. That's it exactly," Polly said.

"But I raised you to want the same things that I want," Lord Springdale said.

"No, Father. You raised me to be a strong, independent woman who thinks for herself, and makes her own decisions. That's not at all the same thing."

Lord Springdale stopped to evaluate what his daughter had just admitted. "And this is what you want? Marriage to a shop owner? Life outside the life of the nobility?"

Polly focused on Ethan and smiled. It was important that he understood without a doubt how much she meant the words she was about to say. "Yes, Papa. This is exactly what I want. Sir Ethan is without a doubt the man I want to be with for the rest of my life. Working at his side for the rest of my life is exactly what I wish to do. And watching our children grow into adults who are as happy as we are now is all I can ask from life."

"Then there is nothing else for me to say," he said.

"You could wish us well. That would be something I would appreciate hearing."

"Very well, Pauline. I wish you well. I wish you a long and happy life with the man you have chosen."

Polly rose from her chair, went to her father, and kissed his cheek. "Thank you, Papa."

Lord Springdale stood, then wrapped his arms around his daughter and hugged her. "I love you, sweetheart."

"I know you do. And I love you."

Their friends and family stayed for a while longer, and they relived the events of the past week. They made plans to tour the estate the queen had given them as a wedding present. And they had one final celebratory drink before everyone headed home.

Polly bade her father a good night and told him that Ethan would walk her home in just a little while. When they were finally alone, Ethan took her in his arms and kissed her.

Every time he kissed her, Polly was reminded of just how much she loved him. She was reminded of how fortunate she was to have found someone as perfect as he was.

Ethan lifted his mouth from hers. "I still can't believe everything that happened this week," he said. "You know that the queen only made me a knight because it was something your father asked her to do."

"No. Father would never have asked her to knight you. That's not something he would do. The queen made you a knight of the realm because you jumped in front of her and saved her from being killed."

"Then the only reason she gave us an estate worth so much as a wedding present was because your father asked her to."

Polly stood on her tiptoes and kissed him. He was the humblest and most modest man she'd ever met. He didn't realize what a hero he was. It wasn't every man who would have the courage to dive in front of bullet to save his queen.

"What other reason could she possibly have had for doing what she did?" he asked.

"Well," Polly said, wrapping her arms around Ethan and placing her cheek against his chest. "You might be right when you say Father was the reason she made you a knight and gifted us with an enviable estate."

"You aren't making any sense, Polly. If he didn't ask her to do those things, why did she do them?"

"Didn't you hear the queen when she made you a knight of the realm?"

Ethan looked at her with a confused expression on his face.

"To quote Her Majesty, she told Father, 'Your requirements have now been met. Your daughter has a mansion in which to live. A knighted husband to love. And a life of happiness to live.'"

"Doesn't that mean that your father asked her to give you those things?"

Polly smiled. "What if instead of Father asking her to knight you and give us the Palmerton Estate, he'd complained because you didn't have a title and couldn't even provide a home for us to live in? So Father asked Her Majesty to help him find a wealthy, titled member of Society who was looking for a wife. Instead, she made you into what Father had asked her for—a wealthy, knighted member of Society who was looking for a wife."

Ethan smiled, then broke out in riotous laughter. "How ingenious! No wonder your father had such a difficult time announcing his blessing for us to marry. He never thought he'd have to."

"Someday we have to make a special effort to thank Her Majesty. I'm sure my father has never been taken so completely off guard."

"I'm sure he hasn't either. We are indeed indebted to Her Majesty."

"Now, if we can just figure out how to convince Father that we'd rather get married in Willowbrook than in London..." Polly said.

"Perhaps if might be wise if we got married in London, Polly."

"What are you saying, Ethan? I didn't think you'd want to get married there."

"I don't. But I was thinking about your father."

"What about my father?"

"Don't you think he's had to give up enough?" Ethan asked. "He was forced to agree to allow us to marry even though I don't possess any of the qualities he wanted for his daughter. And if we can manage to get our books published, he's going to have to endure the embarrassment of Society knowing his son-in-law and daughter write children's books. And—"

"All right. All right. You've made your point. Perhaps he has made enough concessions. I can give in on this one point."

"That's my girl. I'm so proud of you. Come here," he said, gathering her to him. He lowered his head and pressed his lips to hers. His kisses were filled with a passion that caused her entire body to heat. Then he lifted his lips for the briefest of moments and kissed her again. Finally, when he realized that she was having as difficult a time breathing as he was, he ended their kiss and brought her close to him.

"That isn't fair," she said in a voice that broke.

"What isn't fair?"

"What you do to me. This is another reason we never argue."

"Why?"

"Because of the way you kiss me. Your kisses are so numbing I forget what objections I had to whatever it was we were talking about."

"Oh, I like that," he said. "Maybe I should kiss you again."

Polly lifted her head and locked her gaze with his. "Yes, maybe you should. I think you need to practice a little more."

"Perhaps you are right," he said, then pressed his lips to hers again.

CHAPTER TWENTY

Ethan woke and reached out to find Polly's side of the bed empty. It was amazing how he came to miss her when she was gone. And they had only been married a little more than twelve months. He didn't wonder what it would be like when they were married decades. He knew. It would be the same.

He threw the covers off and made his way to the baby's room. He knew he would find Polly there, and when he opened the door, he did. She was sitting in a rocker with their son in her arms and at her breast. It was the most beautiful sight his mind could conceive.

He knew most Society women didn't choose to feed their babes themselves, but Polly wasn't one of those. She'd told him before Andrew was even born that she would feed him herself.

"Did I wake you?" she asked, lifting her gaze and looking at him. There was a smile on her face.

"I missed you," Ethan said. There was only a single candle lit on the dresser behind her, and it cast her in a golden halo of light. She was beautiful. The most beautiful woman he'd ever seen.

Ethan sat in the chair next to hers. "Is he sleeping?"

"Yes. He fell asleep as soon as he finished feeding."

Ethan reached out, took their son from her outstretched arms, and held him close. Polly turned her head to look at him and gently rocked back and forth in her chair. She wore a look of contentment.

Little Drew, as they lovingly called him, stretched his arms above his head, then fell back into a deep sleep.

"What were you thinking about?" Ethan asked.

"Nothing important," she answered.

"You never think of nothing important. Everything that enters your mind is important. Especially to me."

She smiled at him, and Ethan gazed at the beautiful life they had created. There was nothing so precious in the entire world.

"If you must know, I was thinking about how blessed and perfect every second of our lives has been," she said.

"Even the seconds when I was shot and almost died?"

"Especially those."

Ethan couldn't help but be surprised at her words.

"I look back on that time and realize how blessed I was that you survived. Almost losing you made me realize how much I truly loved you, and how impossible it would have been to live without you. It made me realize how short life is, and how important love is."

Ethan couldn't help but smile. "For thinking about nothing, you sure had a lot in your mind."

"It's a habit of mine."

"Yes, it is." He got to his feet and put their son back in his bed. "Remind me again what we're doing tonight," he said, then pulled Polly from her chair and sat down again, but this time with her on his lap.

"You know perfectly well what we're doing tonight. We're having everyone over for dinner to celebrate."

"Oh, is it a special occasion?"

Polly laughed, then nestled closer to Ethan with her head on his chest beneath his chin. "Yes, Ethan. It's a very special occasion. We're going to introduce our family to our newest family member. We're going to introduce everyone to Tommy Turtle—*The Turtle Who Loved to Dance*."

"Oh," Ethan teased. "It slipped my mind."

"It most certainly did not," Polly said. "You were so excited when the books arrived that you couldn't have forgotten."

"No," he said, kissing his wife. "I didn't forget. How could I? You've watched the post every day to see if the books arrived."

"That was because I had to know when to plan our dinner. I could hardly plan such an event before the books arrived. That would have taken the surprise out of our announcement."

She wrapped her arm around his neck and pulled his head down to hers. When he was within reach, she lifted her mouth and kissed him. "And don't forget to say a special thank you to your father," she said. "If it hadn't been for his efforts on our behalf, the London publishers wouldn't have seen your book."

"Not my book, Polly. *Our* book. My story would have been written on lifeless pages without your drawings."

"Thank you, Ethan. I have to agree with you. And I am quite happy with how the final project turned out."

"You should be. You have a gift, my love."

"A gift that never would have seen the light of day without your stories."

Ethan hugged her tighter. "We make a good team, don't we?" he murmured before lowering his head and kissing her again.

"Yes, we do," she said, answering his kiss.

"What about your father?" he asked. "How do you think he will take the news of his daughter painting pictures of dancing animals then putting them in a children's book where the whole of Society can see them?"

"I expect him to be mortified. But he will get over it. That is why I chose a large event to introduce him to what we've done."

Ethan laughed. "Who do you suppose Drew will take after— me with storytelling, or you with drawing?"

"I don't care what he excels at," Polly answered, "as long as it's what he loves doing."

"Which reminds me," Ethan said, rising to his feet with Polly still in his arms. "I know what I love doing," he said, carrying his wife back to their bedroom. He placed her on the bed and came down over her. "And I think I should practice what I love doing so I become more proficient at it."

"Except I'm not sure how you can get more proficient. You're already perfect."

"And so are you," Ethan replied, as he took her in his arms to prove it.

About the Author

Laura Landon taught high school for ten years before leaving the classroom to open her own ice-cream shop. As much as she loved serving up sundaes and malts from behind the counter, she closed up shop after penning her first novel. Now she spends nearly every waking minute writing, guiding her heroes and heroines to find their happily ever afters.

She is the author of more than a dozen historical novels, including SILENT REVENGE, INTIMATE DECEPTION, and her newest Montlake Romance release, INTIMATE SURRENDER.

Her books are enjoyed by readers around the world.